PURSUIT!

Hogan stuck his head out of the Jeep's window. Clicking the AK-47 into automatic, he aimed it at the car behind and squeezed the trigger.

There was an ominous metal click. "It's empty," Hogan said accusingly.

"It constantly runs out of pellets. A very unreliable weapon."

"It wouldn't if you didn't keep firing until the clip was empty," Hogan growled to Brom as he pressed down on the gas pedal.

"No, not yet," Brom insisted. Puzzled, Hogan eased up on the gas.

Brom swung open the car door and leaned out, ignoring the spray of bullets. In his hand he grasped the small battle ax. With a fierce grin, he aimed the weapon and flung it. Traveling in an easy spiral, the ax turned end over end and smashed into the pursuing vehicle, shattering the safety glass into a thousand spiderwebs.

Instinctively, the driver of the sedan ducked and lost control of the vehicle, and the car went suddenly out of control. Swerving to the right, it smashed through the guardrail, then hung in midair for a brief moment....

Forbidden Region

WARRIORS
TIME

David North

A GOLD EAGLE BOOK FROM
WORLDWIDE®

TORONTO • NEW YORK • LONDON • PARIS
AMSTERDAM • STOCKHOLM • HAMBURG
ATHENS • MILAN • TOKYO • SYDNEY

With gratitude to my wonderfully patient
editor, Eva Hicks, and the enthusiastic,
supportive creative management team who
made this vision a reality

First edition August 1991

ISBN 0-373-63602-4

FORBIDDEN REGION

Forbidden Region

PROLOGUE

James Mattoon Holaday leaned over the controls of the Bell AH-l Huey Cobra and glanced down at the desertlike landscape spread out beneath the helicopter.

"The community below is Harwood," the tall, stately man with trim, steel gray hair announced. "This helicopter is courtesy of the United States Air Force," he added, looking at his associate, General Soong.

As a retired air force general, Holaday had found it easy to convince the air force to assign a helicopter for his personal use whenever he needed one.

"You know our plans. The plant here processes very low-grade radioactive material into a gas—uranium hexafluoride. The gas is shipped to a government processing plant where it's turned into high-grade nuclear fuel. But that's done somewhere else, far away from Harwood."

Soong turned his head away from the ground and studied the face of his host.

"So it would be difficult even for a group of determined terrorists to attack the plant and cause many deaths."

"On the contrary, when uranium hexafluoride gas mixes with air, it forms a highly toxic gas which kills on contact."

A third passenger, an immaculately dressed man in his late sixties, kept observing the community through the helicopter window. "How many people live in Harwood?"

Holaday stared at the neatly dressed man. Turner Witherspoon had retired from his post as a senior officer in the Australian military ten years earlier as part of a deal with his government, who agreed not to expose his part in a right-wing attempt to take over the country.

Holaday asked the hard-faced man sitting behind him, "Sergeant Becker, what's the population of Harwood?"

Ex-Sergeant Arnold Becker, military crew cut and steel-hard face, opened a loose-leaf notebook and turned the pages. "Six hundred workers, support personnel, and their families, sir," he replied in the precise voice of a career soldier. "A total population of two thousand, sir."

The Australian became pale. "Do they all have to die?"

Holaday shook his head. The Australian had been reluctant since he had first been contacted.

Holaday regretted that Llewellyn Hazelford, the British member of the group, was not present. Witherspoon and Hazelford had attended Sandhurst at the same time. But Lew Hazelford was standing by in New York, waiting for the signal to carry out his part of the initial actions.

So it was up to Holaday to convince the Australian to join them.

"Like the United States and Canada, Australia is a prime target for Communist anarchists. Your country has large quantities of nuclear ore which these terrorists would like to seize and use as blackmail against the rest of the world. The way to stop them is to go over our weak governments and strike against them before they can destroy the free world. You remember what Father Vigilante said. He's very, very rich, highly intelligent and dedicated. He has some great plans for the world, but we have to act."

Holaday paused to search for the right words to convince the Australian to join the group.

"In every war there are civilian casualties, General Witherspoon. As a senior military man, you've had to face that reality many times."

The Australian lapsed into gloomy silence. Holaday gave him time to reflect and looked at the Oriental sitting next to Witherspoon.

General Soong had also been frustrated in his career plans. Lahoun Soong and Holaday went back to the early years of the Vietnam war. In exchange for providing secret landing fields in Laos for Holaday's planes, Soong had gotten free transportation for the raw opium production he had controlled.

That was all past history. As Holaday remembered, the death of Soong's only son in an unauthorized raid by an elite team of American counterinsurgency specialists had devastated Soong and forced him into early retirement from the government.

Since then, he had dedicated his time and the vast sums of money he had accumulated to seek out and destroy the members of the team who had killed his heir—and to reaping profits from his vast poppy fields in the hilly country of northern Laos. Holaday knew all about the profits to be had from opium. Soong and

he had been working together since he retired from the
air force.

Soong had been reluctant to join the group until the
American general had pointed out that one of the team
responsible for his son's death now worked at the
Harwood plant.

"How is your mission coming, General Soong?"

"The Indian general has agreed to join us. As has
the Thai. The North Vietnamese were noncommittal
until I explained that the first target would be in this
country."

"And your personal matter?"

"By this evening, the men I have hired will have
eliminated John Hogan."

Holaday glanced at the Australian again. "So are
you prepared to join us?"

Witherspoon shook his head. "No. Murdering two
thousand innocent civilians is too insane even for me."

"Is it as insane as the bleeding hearts who run our
countries and continue to forgive criminals who kill
and rape out in the open?"

"I'm sorry, General Holaday, but I decline your
invitation."

With a shrug of regret, Holaday nodded to the hard-
faced sergeant sitting on a jump seat in the rear.

Becker took out a 9 mm Steyr automatic pistol fitted with a silencer from under his jacket. Placing it
against the Australian's forehead, he pulled the trigger twice.

Blood seeped from the two neat holes and stained
the otherwise immaculate face and white shirt with
streaks of dark red as the man slumped forward in his
seat.

"I believe it's time to signal our men below to get started," Holaday said calmly.

"Make sure your seat belts are fastened, gentlemen," he called out. "The final war is about to begin."

1

Charley Grisolm had no idea he had just a few hours left to live as he glanced out of his large office window and studied the landscape.

Bathed in the searing July sun, the endless stretches of Texas plains and mountains beyond the electrified cyclone fence looked like the set for a movie about the Badlands. In the haze of heat, grotesque rock formations took on the appearance of prehistoric monsters waiting to pounce on the nuclear processing plant and the nearby town of Harwood.

But relief was in sight. Thick clouds had begun to pile up in the sky. Within a few hours there would be a downpour, and he could already feel the moisture in the usually dry air. Actually, this would bring a greater risk to the plant. It was especially moisture-laden air that posed a great threat should the gas escape from the holding tanks. The gas would become highly toxic. But everything was running smoothly, and there were no danger signs.

The long row of fourteen-ton tanks that were filled with uranium hexafluoride gas glittered like mirrors as they reflected the sun. Grisolm was grateful their toxic contents were enclosed in thick-walled safety. Even the slightest leak of the low-radioactive contents could kill everyone in a two-mile radius of the tank farm.

A row of tankers was scheduled to drain the huge metal containers the following day and transport the contents to the next step in the nuclear fuel cycle—a government processing plant where the gas would be converted into the high-radioactive pellets to fuel nuclear power plants.

Everything looked normal. He glanced up at the Bell helicopter cruising overhead. He'd been informed that some Texas State officials were showing off the area to visiting businessmen.

Grisolm idly wondered what kind of businesses they were in when his thoughts were interrupted by the ringing of the telephone. The forty-year-old security chief at the Harwood Nuclear Processing Plant smiled as he recognized the voice on the other end. His friend and sergeant in Vietnam, John Hogan, also known as Black Jack Hogan.

"Hey, Black Jack, what are you doin' back in the States?"

Hogan had been living in a Cambodian Buddhist temple since the war had ended. It was a long story, and Grisolm was aware he didn't know the half of it.

"Had to go to Washington for my annual physical."

"Yeah? I didn't know that they insisted on Vietnam vets getting physicals."

The voice on the other end didn't reply, but Grisolm was used to Hogan's silence. Like his Apache ancestors, the tall, powerfully built man had always been closemouthed, even back when Grisolm had served under him as part of the special counterinsurgency team government intelligence had organized to deal with situations the United States government couldn't be involved in officially.

Gossip among the half-dozen members of the C.I. team who had survived the war was that Hogan still worked for the government as an intelligence officer. What he was doing living in a Cambodian temple had puzzled all of them.

Grisolm filled the silence with a question. "Where are you now?"

"Arizona, up near Prescott."

Grisolm knew that Hogan had been raised in the Grand Canyon state on a small ranch, near an Apache reservation. He remembered something else Black Jack had told him.

"I thought your folks were dead."

"They are. But I got some kin on my mother's side. Thought I'd stop by and catch up on family gossip."

Grisolm wondered if Hogan had heard the latest news about their group. "You hear about Buck Hernandez?"

The slight Hispanic from Chicago had been a member of their team—always cracking jokes about the difference in size between himself and the sergeant who led them.

"Larry O'Brien called from Seattle to tell me. If I didn't know better, I'd swear somebody was out to get us. Somebody killed Papagalous out in Los Angeles two months ago. Then Sven Peterson foolishly tripped and fell out of a hotel room window in Minneapolis. Now Hernandez. Hell, Black Jack, that only leaves O'Brien, you and me out of the squad."

"There's only two of us left. O'Brien was reported killed in a car accident last night. So be extra careful. I don't believe in coincidences."

Grisolm was stunned by the news. "Actually Sally and the kids and I are leaving tonight on a month-long leave back to Arkansas to visit our families. She hates me keeping guns around the kids. But I think I'll keep my 9 mm handy in the car."

"Whatever you do, keep your eyes open. I'd give you a number to call me if there's trouble, but I'll be leaving for Cambodia tomorrow morning."

Grisolm looked up at the clock on the wall. "Gotta go, sarge. Time to fax another report to the watchdogs over in Fort Bliss. If I'm late, they'll airlift a platoon of soldiers here to see what's wrong and my ass will be grass."

JOHN HOGAN sped north, pushing the Jeep Cherokee to its limit. He could feel the engine of the sturdy four-wheeler working harder as the highway grades became steeper.

Moving past the long rows of eighteen-wheelers that struggled their way up the long stretches, Hogan tried to concentrate on the scenery. It was the familiar landscape of his youth. The saguaro cactus, arroyos and cholla of the vast Valley of the Sun surrendered to the mesquite trees of the foothills. He studied the rows of mesas across the vast canyon and the stands of yucca, pine and blue spruce that popped up between patches of cactus, agaves and manzanita shrubs. But not even the vivid scenery of his childhood could stop him from thinking about his conversation with Chuck Grisolm.

GRISOLM WAS the only one living of the ten men he had led on secret intelligence missions. Five had died in Indochina, and four of the quintet that had left Indochina alive had met with accidents since they'd been discharged.

Hogan was positive that it was more than mere coincidence. Someone was behind the deaths of his Vietnam team.

He had said as much to Hiram Wilson at Walter Reed Hospital after his annual physical.

Wilson's response had been brief. "You're paranoid."

It was a favorite word of the White House intelligence aide whenever his field agent had instincts about situations or people.

"Maybe," Hogan replied, "but I've been right a helluva lot more times than I've been wrong."

He wanted to take a leave of absence and conduct his own investigation, but Wilson vetoed the idea, promising to have his own FBI and police contacts check into the deaths again.

Instead the soft-spoken intelligence aide to the President suggested his key field agent take a vacation before returning to the Cambodian Buddhist sanctuary Hogan called home.

"It wouldn't do your body any harm to give it a rest for a week or so," commented Colonel Martingdale, the bald senior medical officer who supervised the examination.

Hogan was about to argue with the medical man, when Wilson stopped him. "Change that from a suggestion to an order," he said icily.

The burly man became sarcastic. "Where am I supposed to take this vacation?"

Wilson ignored the question as he carefully took out one of the Cuban cigars he smoked and clipped the end with a sterling silver cigar clipper. Lighting the other end with a wooden match, he looked up at Hogan and smiled.

"I think a visit home would be a nice gesture," he said.

The medical officer became alert. "Where would home be?"

When Hogan didn't reply, Wilson carefully studied him. "Your family still have the ranch outside of Prescott, Arizona?"

Hogan shook his head. "It was sold after the folks died."

"How about your relatives?"

The half-clad muscular man sitting on the examining table thought about it.

"I've got some distant cousins. And my grandfather. They still live on the Apache reservation out there."

Hiram Wilson took a slow puff on his long, tan-colored cigar and let the smoke from his mouth waft toward the ceiling.

"I'll book you a flight," he said.

Hogan tried to argue with him. "I could be a lot of help in trying to find out who's behind the deaths of my men."

Wilson smiled. "Enjoy your visit with your family," he said, then turned and walked out of the room before Black Jack could continue.

THE STEADY DRONE of the engines took his thoughts back to the past. He realized that this was the first time he would be returning to the place of his birth since he had left for Vietnam fifteen years ago.

Not exactly his birthplace, Hogan reminded himself. The large, lonely ranch he had been raised on had been auctioned after the death of his parents.

Where he was heading was the Apache Reservation north of Prescott where the last of his family—his mother's father—still lived. Hogan had spent many happy days sitting at the feet of his grandfather, listening to stories of his days as an Apache warrior, fighting in the last great battles against the white settlers at the side of such fearsome leaders as Geronimo and Mangus Coloradas.

As a child, Hogan was hypnotized by his grandfather's vivid tales of bloody combat. Now, as an adult who was almost forty, he wondered how much of it was invention to entertain an impressionable, blue-eyed grandchild, and how much was fact.

It really didn't matter. The days of the Indian wars were long over. And now Wise Crow was a shaman— a holy man—and in his eighties. As he thought about it, Hogan was glad Wilson had demanded he take a few days off before he flew back to Cambodia. He had a need to see the last of his family one more time and come to peace with his Native American heritage. Wise Crow would probably not live through another winter.

Except for the handful of eighteen wheelers that passed him in both directions, there was little traffic on the highway.

Black Jack glanced into his rearview mirror. A large luxury sedan was coming up behind him.

Tourists, he decided, as the car passed him on the left. He casually turned his head toward the passing car to glance at the passengers and saw the hard, dead expressions on the faces of the men inside. His relaxed posture vanished and he came alert. These were professional. Hired killers. And judging by the way they were studying him, he was their target.

There was a glint of sun shining on metal in the hands of one of them.

Hogan recognized it for what it was. An automatic weapon. An Uzi or TEC-9, Hogan decided as he twisted the wheel of his Jeep and turned toward the car.

He didn't waste time worrying about the brand. It didn't matter. Any one of them could kill.

That someone was trying to kill him didn't come as a surprise. Since the Cambodian monks had found him near death after a Khmer Rouge ambush and nursed him back to life, Hogan had been the target of determined assassins. But that episode had also brought a strange ally into his life—one he wouldn't talk about for fear he would be considered out of his mind.

Even his own government had marked him for death because he knew too much about secret missions whose existence had officially been denied. He had been pronounced unstable by government medical examiners, and only Hiram Wilson, who had been his CIA control in Indochina during the war, was able to rescue him.

As the newly appointed White House intelligence aide, he tagged the former counterinsurgency special-

ist as his field agent and suggested he return to the
Cambodia temple to live between assignments.

Hogan preferred living there, rather than to survive
in the frantic civilized world in which he no longer fit.
At least no one tried to harm him there, with the possible exception of the elderly abbot of the monastery,
Mok Seng, who had decided the American needed to
be taught the correct way to live and fight.

Hogan had accumulated a great number of enemies since he had accepted Wilson's offer. What he
didn't know was which of them had hired the gunmen
chasing him.

Over the rush of wind slamming against his car, he
could hear the soft thud of slugs glancing off his vehicle. The chunks of hot lead cut grooves in the skin
of his car as he kept trying to present as small a pro-
file as he could. Before he was done with it, he suspected the rental agency would be getting back a
vehicle scarred by streaks of searing lead slugs.

He jammed down on the brakes. The driver of the
Lincoln did the same and almost slammed into the side
of Hogan's vehicle, then swerved away to avoid a collision.

Hogan started to reach for the 9 mm Beretta 92F he
usually carried in his waistband holster, then remembered he had left it at the temple in Cambodia when he
flew to the United States. The only weapon he had was
the sharp long-bladed knife he had received as a gift,
but it was packed in the duffel bag.

The green sign along the side of the four-lane interstate announced that the Prescott exit was three miles
away. There was only one chance, Black Jack decided.

To outrun them until...until what? He wasn't sure.

He didn't know if his other-worldly help would show up. He had expected help in the form of the red-bearded warrior. Usually Brom had appeared whenever Hogan was in danger, but there was no sign of him now.

He shoved the gas pedal to the floor and raced for the exit. Through his rearview mirror he could see the large sedan trying to catch up with him.

A SHIMMERING CLOUD began to form in a corner of the huge palace bedroom, but the red-bearded warrior who lay on the cushions spread around the floor was too lost in his thoughts to notice it.

As exhausted as he was, Brom couldn't sleep. For more than an hour, he had stared at the ceiling of the bedroom where his late father and mother had lived before their deaths.

As the new ruler of Kalabria, Brom had much to cope with—especially since Mondlock the Knower had vanished. Mondlock had served as friend, surrogate father, advisor, and substitute ruler of Kalabria when Brom got fed up with the boring intrigue of politics.

There was so much to get done. The capitol city of Tella was being restored from the wreckage the hordes of savage invaders from across the Great Eastern Desert had left behind. Each detail required his personal attention.

Now there was a new problem. For the past two weeks, thousands of pilgrims had slipped across the Kalabrian border, heading toward the Forbidden Region where a strange prophet who had come from some land past the Great Eastern Desert had promised that the great god Ost was waiting for them.

Brom had sent skilled orators to try to convince them to return to their homelands. But their efforts had been fruitless.

And now even Kalabrians were joining the ranks of the wanderers.

Mondlock would know how to handle the situation. The pilgrims were not soldiers, but half-starved men, women and children seeking some promised paradise. Convincing them to return to their own lands required diplomacy, not military force.

But Mondlock the Knower was still gone. He was supposed to have returned to Tella weeks ago from his annual trek into the Forbidden Region where the all-powerful creator of life and energy resided. The wise man was, in addition to everything else, one of the handful of Knowers who served Ost as his priests.

For more than a week Brom had led a troop of his personal guard into the Forbidden Region to find him, but it seemed as though the desert had swallowed him and left no trace of where he had gone.

Mora had been joyous at his return last night. The lithe but curvaceous woman had practically dragged him to the bedchamber before he could even strip off his armor.

As usual they had come together in a heated embrace. He glanced at the soft, blond hair sprawled across the pillow next to him. Mora was asleep, a pleased smile on her face.

As he lifted his head and studied her face, now softened by slumber, he was glad she spent the night with him. For all the arguments they had exchanged over the years, Mora was the only person he trusted, aside from Mondlock.

He looked at the lithe form, relaxed in sleep, that pressed against him. Some had warned that she couldn't bear many children. Her body was too thin, her hips not wide enough.

He knew they were wrong. She had the body of a dancer, the strength of a warrior, and the soul of a good mother.

There was a bonding between them that was more powerful than their strenuous physical encounters. He planned to ask her to bond with him for life in front of the Gods and his people.

Even though they hadn't discussed it, he suspected she knew. Women had a way of knowing such things, especially a woman like Mora.

Brom closed his eyes and tried to sleep, then decided rest would not come to him.

He was quietly sliding toward the edge of the bed when he heard a soft voice.

"Mondlock will return."

Brom turned. Mora smiled and reached out a bare arm toward him.

"Something has happened to him," Brom said, his voice edged with his concern.

"Not sleeping won't bring him back," she said, then lifted her head from the pillow and looked past Brom.

"This must be the season of difficulty," she commented, still looking over his shoulder.

Brom swiveled around and saw the shimmering cloud moving toward him. It was the sign that the strange battler from another world needed his assistance.

"Hogan is in trouble again," he grumbled under his breath, as he jumped from the bed and moved to the array of weapons propped against the wall. His "howling sword," a long, heavy double-edged blade, stood next to a small battle-ax and the deadly fire-stick Hogan had left in his keeping.

On the table nearby was a jeweled scabbard that held his krall—the long-bladed knife that all adult males wore in Kalabria.

Brom could remember clearly their first meeting, when he had thought Hogan was a reincarnation of Komar, the God of Vengeance. Then he'd learned that Hogan was like himself, a man and a great warrior.

As Mondlock The Knower had explained it, because they had both come close to death, to the visit the gates of the underworld at the same time, somehow their spirits had become intertwined.

Ever since then, the appearance of the shimmering cloud became the signal that one of them needed the help of the other.

Even after all this time, Brom couldn't comprehend how two men from different worlds could become virtual twins. He suspected Hogan understood it no better than himself. But however it happened, each appeared at the first sign of danger to the other and fought as if he was fighting for his own life.

Mora sat up and pulled the covers against her milk-white flesh.

"Remind Hogan that Astrah waits for him here," she said as Brom was trying to decide which of the weapons he should carry.

Astrah, glowing and pink-frost lovely, had chosen Hogan as her mate on a previous encounter. As was the Kalabrian tradition, she waited patiently for her man to return to her between campaigns.

Brom nodded absentmindedly and made a decision to take all his weapons. He glanced at Mora to reassure her of his speedy return, then heard her soft laugh as she studied him.

"Is something wrong?"

Mora began to giggle. "My Lord, maybe it would be better if you wore some clothes."

The Kalabrian ruler looked down at himself. He was naked. Muttering something about women who like to laugh at their men, he slipped into a pair of wide black pants and a loose fitting cotton tunic, then pulled on a pair of soft leather boots.

As he gathered up his weapons, Mora slipped out of the bed. "Tell Hogan it's a good thing he didn't put himself in danger several hours ago or he would have had me to deal with," she called out in a lilting voice.

"I'll tell him," Brom promised, waving to her as he stepped into the center of the bright cloud.

AFTER HANGING UP, Charley Grisolm flipped on the radio and leaned back in his chair. The radio on his desk was playing country-and-western music broadcast from a small FM station in Odessa.

Behind him were a row of television monitors, but he was tired of staring at them. The plant was secure from attack. The remote communications network the Nuclear Regulatory Commission had insisted the company install would immediately alert the military. Specially trained soldiers from Fort Bliss would descend on the site in less than two hours.

In addition, there were a dozen armed security guards who reported to him, keeping close watch on the top-secret plant each shift. All of them had called in with the required hourly inspection reports.

He glanced at the clock on the wall above the television screens. Eleven fifty-six.

Soon the noon whistle would blow and the workers would pour out and into their cars to go to lunch. Some generally drove to their homes in nearby Harwood while others patronized the fast-food outlets along the highway to town.

There used to be a cafeteria right in the plant. But the workers avoided it as if they somehow feared contamination of the food. Six months after Grisolm joined the company, the cafeteria had closed.

He understood the uneasiness of the employees. Even though he knew the chance of a leak in the tanks was extremely small, he still felt uncomfortable being this close to them. Accidents did happen and workers did die. Tensely he glanced at the meters in front of him. Each of them was connected to a sensitive device that could detect the most minute amount of escaping gas.

As usual, the meters indicated everything was normal.

He let out a small sigh. After today he would stop worrying. In a few hours he'd load Sally and the kids into their station wagon and head east to visit the folks. He'd made up his mind to tell her that he wasn't planning to return.

He turned his head and glanced at the rows of streets that ran in checkerboard fashion three miles east of the huge concrete-reinforced plant. They'd miss Harwood and the friends they had made during their three-year stay. But it was time to move somewhere else.

Before he could think about it any more, the phone on his desk rang. The call was on time. It had to be Peter Arbinot, the new head of the Nuclear Regulatory Commission safety inspection team at the plant, making his telephone rounds.

"Grisolm," he said crisply into the receiver.

Charley recognized Arbinot's stiff, formal-sounding voice on the other end.

"Would you mind waiting in your office? There's one more thing I need from you."

Grisolm glanced at the clock. His replacement was due to be driving through the front gate any minute.

"Sure. I'm not going anyplace," Charley said, then hung up.

Making a face at the prospect of seeing Arbinot, he reminded himself that the man was just a typical example of the bureaucrats the government sent in to snoop at the Harwood plant.

As he gathered his reports, Grisolm checked the wall clock. Four more hours, and his vacation would start. In forty minutes he could turn the office over to Tony Pelligreed, take a shower, change clothes and go home.

On the radio Simon and Garfunkel were singing. "Homeward bound . . ."

Chuck smiled at the lyrics. That's just where he and the family would be this afternoon.

He was so deeply engrossed that he didn't hear the door open.

"Thank you for waiting."

Grisolm looked up. It was Peter Arbinot, though it took a minute to connect the voice to the apparition before him.

He stared at the contamination suit the Nuclear Regulation Agency inspector was wearing. "Is something wrong?"

From outside he heard a strange sound. He looked through the window and saw three men in contamination suits firing automatic weapons at the storage tanks. Even though it was invisible, he knew that the deadly gas was rushing through the ruptures in the metal containers.

For a moment he was too stunned to do anything but look on in disbelief at the horror the three men had just let loose on Harwood.

THE INVISIBLE GAS quickly spread through the community.

On Knowles Lane, Sally Grisolm walked out of the air-conditioned house. Her son Timmy was supposed to put his toys away in the garage and come right back. There was still a lot of packing to do before Charley came home and helped load up the family station wagon.

She started to call out for the six-year-old boy, then saw him lying facedown on the grass near the garage.

For a moment she thought he was playacting, then she felt the burning in her throat and eyes. The burning moved down through her entire body and she wanted to scream from the awful pain. But before the first sound could come out of her mouth, she crumpled in a dead heap.

Workers leaving for lunch walked out of the plant and dropped to the ground, one after another, as though felled by an invisible hand.

The inside of Simpson's Supermarket was a scene from a nightmare. Bodies of checkout girls and customers were everywhere, twisted bodies with faces still frozen in silent screams.

As GRISOLM SAW the men shooting at the filled tanks, a stray bit of information clicked in his head. It was something the plant manager had told him when he'd signed on as security chief.

"The only time there's any chance of a real disaster is if the gas mixes with moist air. Then it can kill anyone who breathes it almost instantly."

He thought of Sally and the kids, the inhabitants of those familiar streets, and was galvanized into action. Swiftly turning back, he yanked his drawer to grab his 9 mm Glock 7 automatic pistol.

"Hit the alarm button," he shouted to Arbinot. "We're being attacked!"

The gray-haired man nodded, then took his hand out of his pocket. He was holding a 9 mm Steyr automatic.

Aiming carefully, he fired three shots into the security man's torso. Grisolm staggered back, and an awful realization dawned on his face.

Arbinot quickly pulled down the plastic-visored hood of the suit and carefully sealed it.

"I know," he replied calmly. "I'm doing the attacking."

But Grisolm no longer heard anything as his body landed with a dull crash.

He was dead.

2

Hogan's Jeep careened down the steep exit road from the interstate. Through his side-view mirror, he could see the pursuit car struggling to keep up.

As he maneuvered a sharp curve, a tandem trailer loomed in front of him. Twisting the wheel of his Jeep, Black Jack narrowly missed a head-on collision.

He glanced up at the rearview mirror. The long sedan was still behind him.

He floored the accelerator, then became aware of a shimmering dimness. He shook his head, trying to clear his vision. But immediately he felt a presence beside him, and heard a snort of disbelief. He glanced to his right.

His fate had caught up to him. The shimmering had faded, and sitting in the front passenger seat was his counterpart from that other dimension, grasping an armful of weapons.

"Welcome aboard," Hogan shouted to Brom as he struggled to prevent his vehicle from running off the narrow road and down the sheer wall of Copper Canyon. "Looks like you're prepared for anything," he added as he saw the variety of combat instruments.

"Except death," Brom yelled back. "Do we need to race so fast?"

"Look behind you."

The red-bearded Kalabrian turned his head. He saw that the large vehicle behind them was filled with men brandishing spitting fire-sticks.

"Why are those men shooting death pellets at us?"

"Because they want to kill us—at least me—I think," Black Jack replied.

"Who is mad at you?"

"I'm not sure."

"You live in a strange world, Hogan. People kill one another for no reason." He looked puzzled. "To think that when I first met you I thought you were one of the gods," he added.

The hammering of hot lead from the automatic weapons against the metal skin of Hogan's vehicle interrupted Brom's comment.

Hogan saw the AK-47 Brom held on his lap. He had given it to the Kalabrian on his last journey there.

"Is that gun loaded?"

Brom shrugged. "It was the last time I fired it."

"Hand it to me," Black Jack ordered.

Brom looked out of his window and stared at the steep mountainside to their right.

"Let me do the fighting," he suggested nervously, "while you try to keep this iron horse from falling down the mountain."

"The gun," Hogan insisted.

Reluctantly Brom handed the automatic weapon over. Hogan slowed down the Jeep and stuck his head out of his window. Clicking the weapon to automatic, he aimed it at the car behind and squeezed the trigger.

The only response was an ominous metallic click.

"It's empty," Hogan said accusingly.

"It constantly runs out of pellets. A very unreliable weapon."

"It wouldn't if you didn't keep firing until the clip was empty," Hogan growled. "You've got to learn to conserve your ammunition."

The American warrior wondered what the next move was. Brom's sword and krall weren't useful except in close combat. Perhaps he could make it to the nearest cutoff, where they could escape on foot.

He pressed down on the gas pedal.

"No, not yet," the Kalabrian insisted.

Puzzled, Black Jack eased up on the gas.

Brom opened his car door and leaned out, ignoring the continuing spray of bullets coming at him. In his hand he grasped the small battle-ax he had brought with him.

With a fierce grin on his face, he aimed the small, metal-headed weapon and flung it. Traveling in an easy spiral like a football, the ax turned end over end and smashed into the windshield of the pursuing vehicle. The safety glass shattered into a thousand spiderwebs held together by the layer of safety bonding in the windshield.

Instinctively the driver of the sedan ducked and lost control of the vehicle.

Suddenly berserk, the car swerved to the right and smashed through the low guardrail, then hung in midair for a brief moment only to plunge down into the canyon far below the highway.

The faint screams of terrified men staring at their impending death soon vanished as the sedan crashed into a stand of jagged boulders and burst into flames.

Hogan pulled his Jeep into one of the runaway-truck bypasses that dotted Interstate 17 and stopped. Getting out, he smiled gratefully at his ally, who got out on the other side.

"If you ever learn how to handle a gun, you'll be a world-class danger."

"It's not my fault the fire-sticks are made so poorly."

Black Jack was confused. "Poorly?"

"They run out of power so quickly. I was leading a troop of my warriors in a battle against a small force of mercenaries who were robbing some of our farmers. My fire-stick was spitting its metal pellets of death at their commanders. Then suddenly it stopped and became silent."

Now Hogan understood. "You ran out of ammunition."

"At a most difficult moment. I had to leap from my horse and duel three of the hired captains."

Hogan had tried to explain that each of the clips he had given Brom contained only 30 rounds of 600-grain ammunition. But the red-headed giant refused to believe that the assault rifle could have any limitations.

"Where'd you get the clip you were just using?"

Brom grinned. "I was carrying another filled container."

Black Jack understood that the Kalabrian was referring to a clip.

"Only a few of the metal pellets were needed to kill the mercenary officers before the rest of their troop turned and ran away," Brom added with a grin as he remembered the incident.

"The clip is empty now," Hogan said, knowing he sounded like a parent reprimanding a child.

"I know." Brom looked guilty, then glanced hopefully at the American. "You wouldn't happen to have more of the containers?"

Black Jack shook his head.

"The next time I come to Kalabria, I'll bring more," he promised, giving up ever making the fierce warrior understand the concept of wasting ammunition.

"Make your visit soon," Brom warned. "Astrah, the temple maiden, is starting to wonder if you have another woman in your world."

Hogan grinned. "You never know."

"I wouldn't make light with your comments. My Mora has been training her to become a dance warrior."

In Kalabria, Brom's country, dance warriors were women whose combined skills at dancing, acrobatics and battling would shame all but the strongest of male warriors.

"Then tell her no," Hogan said hastily. "There is no other woman."

Brom grinned knowingly. "Spoken like a wise man."

"How goes the peace?"

"We have a new plague. Pilgrims have begun to cross our lands, determined to reach the Forbidden Region and search for the great god Ost."

Hogan was puzzled. "Who leads them?"

Brom shook his massive head. "A prophet. No one knows for sure, but some say he looks like the magician Nis, whose powers we have battled."

"He doesn't seem to know when to quit," Black Jack commented.

"There is something in Kalabria he wants. No one is certain what he is seeking."

"Not even the wise man?"

"Yes, Mondlock the Knower would know what Nis is seeking. But he is away."

The two men retrieved their weapons, and Hogan became lost in thought, trying to figure out who had sent the car full of hired killers.

Brom gave Hogan a measuring look. "Is something else wrong?"

Hogan explained about the dead men who had been under his command.

"An enemy from the past," the Kalabrian announced with certainty. "Tell me where to find him."

Black Jack had seen the effect the warrior chief had on his opponents. Even when compared to Hogan, Brom was an imposing figure. Standing at least three inches taller, the visitor from the other-dimension land of Kalabria was an awesome sight.

"I will when I learn who it is," the American promised.

Brom nodded. "Until then, I must go back."

"Why the hurry?"

"Mondlock has not returned from his meditation journey, leaving me to solve the problems of Kalabria by myself. I've had my troops searching unsuccessfully for him through the kingdom. And as I told you, we must deal with those pilgrims streaming across our border daily by the hundreds. It seems there is no turning them back by reasoning. And my love, Mora, is anxious to hold me again."

Vague shimmering filled the air several yards away from the Jeep, and Brom and Hogan clasped forearms. Then the Kalabrian moved toward the mist.

"Thanks for the help," the American shouted.

"Now you owe me, Hogan," the Kalabrian yelled back.

Hogan nodded. He was sure the debt would be paid. And soon.

As he looked at the empty space where Brom had disappeared, he shook his head. He still didn't really understand how the two of them had become attuned to each other, and especially how they could bodily appear in each other's world. It had been explained to Hogan that their spirits had met when they were both at death's door, and that a powerful bonding kept pulling them back together in times of need.

Hogan was a realist, not inclined to believe in such things. But neither could he deny that these things were actually happening.

3

The rambling adobe house with the red tiled roof was set back from the two-lane country road. From the outside the nondescript structure looked like any of the neighboring homes in that part of the Texas Panhandle.

The major difference was inside the house.

One whole wing of the house had been turned into a military communications center.

Only a handful of men and women ever visited the place. With the destruction of the Berlin Wall and the ending of the Cold War, very few people had any interest in the daily activities of a retired air force general.

One of the few visitors to make the long trek to the remote ranch let his body sink down into the softness of the large couch and waited for his host to return.

Lahoun Soong was satisfied. The day had gone well. Harwood no longer existed. Nor did Charles Grisolm.

Now only John Hogan remained alive. And the American general had made arrangements to have him eliminated before he left the country to his foreign headquarters.

Soong looked around the vast private office. The walls were covered with photographs of a tall, stately military officer in the company of a great number of foreign government officials. He studied them for a particular photograph, then found it.

The picture of General Holaday and himself, taken in Vientiane in the seventies. The American had been the deputy commander of American forces in Indochina and he the military head of central Laos forces.

He reflected on what had been the beginning of a profitable association for both men. Soong had provided Holaday's forces with secret landing fields and staging areas in their war on the Communists, as well as scores of undercover soldiers from the warlike Hmong tribesmen who lived in the hills near the Chinese border in the north of the country.

In return the American made sure that Soong's most important export, pure opium, was secretly flown to the United States and Europe aboard military transport planes.

After the war, before the American left for his home, Soong had proposed that they continue their business arrangement.

Their business worked out. Holaday provided warehouse facilities near the Mexican border and got a share of the profits.

The Laotian had been pleased with the vast sums Holaday was earning for him. He'd even given some thought to shutting down the small protection service he had been offering to Indochinese businessmen who now lived in the United States. It required a large number of collectors and enforcers, whom Becker had been helping to recruit for an extra fee.

He didn't mind that Holaday had left the day-to-day running of the business to his mistress, Valerie, and Sergeant Becker, his right-hand man. Soong knew them both. The woman had been Holaday's aide, a major in the American air force and was tougher than most men the Laotian had known.

But everything changed when Holaday had invited him to join the elite group of generals.

In the beginning he had been reluctant to get involved in anything that would take him from his business. But now Soong could taste the power that was almost his again. As profitable as the businesses he had established had been, he missed the excitement of controlling the lives of thousands of men. The aphrodisiac of power was a thousand times more stimulating than running a chain of brothels in Laos and Thailand, his opium business or his protection services.

If everything moved along on the planned schedule, he would be receiving a plea from the Laotian government in a few weeks—as would the others of the group from their countries—to return and save his native country from the anarchists who were using threats of wholesale destruction to gain control of Laos.

Then they would work together after they took over their governments and make plans for the future of the world.

There would be arguments about who should chair the committee. They would probably settle on someone from a Third World country. Someone like himself.

The thought pleased him, and he was smiling slightly to himself when Holaday strolled in, carrying a couple of glasses. Glancing at his guest, the retired general set down the drinks.

"One of my men heard a bulletin on the radio about a nuclear accident in Harwood, Texas," Holaday said, sounding satisfied.

Soong nodded his head approvingly.

"Good. And soon the men I have hired will complete the avenging of my son's honor."

For ten years he had waited for this moment, ever since Hogan and his band had slipped across the border from Vietnam and blown up the plant where he had been extracting the opium from the poppies.

Nine of his men had died in the battle, including his son. Now he had almost completed his vow of revenging his heir's murder. All of the invading team was dead, except for their leader.

In a soft, humble voice, the Oriental added a note of gratitude. "I thank you for finding out where the hated Hogan is."

Holaday had told Sergeant Becker to have his contacts keep a tab on Hogan's planned movements. Colonel Martingdale, a senior medical officer at Walter Reed Hospital, in Washington, D.C., reported that their target had come in for his annual checkup and was on his way to the Apache reservation near Prescott, Arizona.

"Glad to help out an old friend," the lanky retired officer said with a casual wave of his hand.

"Things are moving even faster than I would have predicted," Holaday went on. "According to the news reports, the governor of Texas is sending in the National Guard—all decked out in decontamination suits—to evacuate anybody who is still alive. The White House blamed the disaster on carelessness. And several dozen senators are demanding an immediate investigation to see if the manufacturers of the storage tanks are to blame."

He lowered his frame into a large easy chair.

"Watch the American people turn on the fuzzy-brained liberals who keep picketing nuclear sites after our message is released to the press," he added.

"I think the public outcry will increase," Soong commented, "after our Russian counterpart completes his part of the mission."

"Agreed. And with each explosion, the demand for a change in leadership will increase," the retired general said. "I have arranged to appear on network television after the Eastern European incidents to demand that the administration act before they surrender the country to anarchists."

"And you will be the obvious choice to take matters in hand."

Soong picked up his drink and lifted his glass into the air. "I propose a toast to the terrorists of the world. And to those who will stop them from destroying nuclear installations."

The toast was interrupted by the stern-faced Sergeant Becker. He looked at the guest.

"There's a call for you, General."

"You can take it in the den if you prefer privacy," Holaday suggested.

Soong smiled gratefully and left the room.

"And, sir," Becker added, "Miss Wilding called from Washington, D.C., again."

Holaday's face revealed his irritation. Valerie was becoming a nuisance.

The sergeant coughed discreetly. "One more thing, General. Miss Wilding said she planned to fly out here if she didn't hear from you by tomorrow night."

Something would have to be done about Valerie, Holaday acknowledged to himself, then looked meaningfully at the sergeant.

"Do you have any contacts who could handle Miss Wilding?"

The stone-faced noncom understood.

"Of course," he said, and withdrew from the room.

It wouldn't do for a spiteful Valerie to start talking to the authorities just as his vision of a perfect world, one that he helped rule, was about to become a reality.

In a few minutes Soong stormed back into the office. His face had a formidable look.

Holaday studied his expression. "No success with Hogan?"

"Yes, thanks to the incompetents hired to do the job."

"I can ask Becker to line up some professionals," the American offered.

Soong listened, expressionless. He didn't bother mentioning that Becker had actually recruited the first group of hit men.

Holaday supervised the distribution to major wholesalers of shipments of opium, and the sergeant served as a recruiter of enforcement talent whenever a drug dealer or protection client showed reluctance to pay promptly.

"I would appreciate that," he said politely.

Holaday went to the door and gestured for the sergeant to join them. He explained the problem, and Becker gave him a quick smile.

"My friends said that they could resolve your problem in Washington, D.C.," he said casually, then vanished from the room.

Holaday turned to his guest.

"What do you propose to do if the second group also fails?"

Soong tapped his fingers on the desk as he thought, then said, "I need to make a call."

As he waited for someone to answer the phone, the Laotian weighed what little he knew about the American agent's life-style. Hogan preferred to spend his time between missions in some sanctuary in Cambodia. There were no direct flights from the United States to the small Communist-dominated country. The American would have to enter through Hanoi or Bangkok.

There was little likelihood that Hogan would risk entering Vietnam. No, Soong decided. He would first land in Bangkok, then continue his journey into Cambodia.

From the United States the main gateways to Thailand were from Los Angeles and San Francisco.

He would have both of them covered.

A familiar voice answered. "Lon Nol Importing Company."

"This is Soong." During the brief exchange, he made it clear what he wanted.

Then, turning from the telephone, he glanced at Holaday. "I will have the money delivered to you in two days. And now it is time for me to return to Vientiane before some ambitious drug agent discovers I am in your country."

The two faced each other and exchanged a warm handshake.

"I will be waiting for your call. It has been a long time since my government was properly run."

"CALL ME as soon as you know that John Hogan is eliminated," the blond man said quietly in response to the report from the retired air force general.

He set the phone down and narrowed his almond-shaped eyes as he gazed through the study window at the vast Aegean Sea. There was a deceptive calm on the water that could change in seconds to a violent storm.

It was just like life for the inhabitants of this strange world.

They were so easy to convince. Even he had been surprised how quickly this James Holaday begged to do his bidding. The hunger for power among these creatures was amazing. They would destroy anyone, do anything for it.

He did not relish being here. But it was no worse than the other world. Both were filled with primitive beings.

There was only one thing they had that interested him—supplies of the glowing rocks he needed to sustain his existence.

This was his second time in both worlds. His first exploration produced little of the energy stones, thanks to the incompetence of those he had recruited to carry out his orders.

He had assumed a physical form in which to communicate with the beings of the two worlds, and along with it the name Nis.

Disappointed with the poor results of his first visit, he had left to explore other worlds. With no success.

He was back. But this time he would succeed in his search.

He retained the form he had used on the early visit, but changed his identity to make his plans seem more palatable to those he recruited. Now he was called Father Vigilante and passed himself off as a rich, reclusive visionary.

He needed to discover large deposits of the glowing rocks soon. He had enough energy to sustain his existence for six more months at most.

Preliminary exploration of both worlds had indicated potentially large supplies of the rare energy rocks. But there was still the problem of large populations to eliminate before he could search for them safely.

From previous experience, only a scant handful of the inhabitants were not so easily convinced. The first was on this world—the bullheaded warrior named Hogan, who had frustrated his search for the glowing rocks before. The second was the huge red-haired primitive who called himself Brom and ruled a small country on the second target for the glowing rocks. They had presented a real obstacle especially because they had acquired a way to traverse barriers of time and dimension.

There would be only some minor details to handle once the rocks had been located. Crucial to his success was the elimination of the surrounding populations so that there was no threat of interruption while he began the process of absorbing the energy.

Then he could resume his search on the thousands of still-unexplored worlds, and assure the continued existence of the Guardians, the most perfect of all species—of which he was the last.

4

Black Jack Hogan knew he was dreaming.

Images paraded before him fleetingly, full of color and sound. Then he felt a hand on his arm, and a voice said urgently, "There is a telephone call for you."

Hogan mumbled something, but he was being shaken awake. Reluctantly he rubbed the sleep from his eyes and sat up. This was no dream.

"A man named Wilson is calling you from Washington." Now Hogan saw that it wasn't a dream figure but his grandfather, Wise Crow.

He jumped from the small bed and moved quickly to the living room. Perhaps he had some clues at last.

He listened quietly as Wilson told him about Harwood. Before he could reply, the Washington official gave him an order. "I want you to keep away. So far as they can determine, the area is still too hot to enter. And from all signs, it was just a tragic accident."

Hogan said nothing. Wilson was right. It was pointless to go, but some instinct prompted that it was more than just an accident.

He glanced through the windows. Outside, the hot Arizona sun continued its incessant scorching of the scant vegetation.

Hogan's suntanned features reflected his anger. Now he was the only one alive. According to the intelligence aide, the so-called accident had occurred less than an hour after Grisolm and he had spoken on the phone.

There was no way Charley and his family could have escaped, and a heaviness settled in his chest and clenched his stomach. He kept pacing around the small room, trying to dissipate the frustration and fury he felt at the news.

He looked around the living room of his grandfather's house. It had been many years since he'd last set foot in here—just before he left for college.

The walls were covered with Apache memorabilia—relics of Wise Crow's bravery as a warrior. He kept staring at the longbow he still remembered his grandfather practicing with when he was a child. Before Wise Crow became a shaman—a holy man—he had been a war chief of his tribe.

Hogan's body quivered with the rage he felt. Suddenly he grabbed the telephone and started to dial a private number at the White House. The number connected to the phone on Wilson's desk.

It started to ring, but Black Jack abruptly hung up before anyone answered.

He clenched his fists as he thought about how the conversation would go. What made him even more angry was that inside he knew Wilson was right in advising him to go back to Cambodia until more information surfaced. There was nothing he could do for Grisolm and his family.

Except find those responsible and make them pay.

Hiram Wilson was his boss. Or **at** least the government official who gave him missions and paid for their successful completion.

More important, the white-haired Southerner was responsible for his still being alive after a decision had been made in Washington to have him eliminated because he was no longer considered stable enough to be trusted with the knowledge of secret military missions he had led in Vietnam. Only Wilson's intervention, as special intelligence aide to the President, had prevented the execution of the decision. In exchange, Hogan agreed to take on those missions to which the American government couldn't admit involvement.

He knew that to some extent Wilson cared about what happened to him. That is, if it didn't interfere with the successful completion of a mission.

Black Jack kept toying with the telephone, trying to decide whether he should go to Harwood or leave for Cambodia as he had originally planned. Slamming his fist down on the table, he made up his mind to continue with the original plan.

The pent-up emotions in him still needed venting. Hogan lifted the longbow and the quiver of hand-crafted arrows from their place of honor on the wall and stepped outside. The leather-faced Indian who was his mother's father was sitting on the front steps, his eyes focused on the vast dry land that made up the Apache reservation.

Wise Crow watched him approach with the bow. "Many brave warriors have been sent to their eternal places with that bow," he grunted. "Many strong animals have been killed to provide meat with it. It has a history of great honor."

"If you object, I'll put it back on the living-room wall," Black Jack said quietly.

"No. But you have not handled such a weapon since you were a small boy."

Hogan smiled. For three years one of the daily exercises his mentor, Mok Seng, had put him through was a grueling drill on the use of the bow.

"Yes, I have, grandfather."

Wise Crow looked surprised.

"I did not know the palefaces for whom you work permitted the use of such weapons."

"They would rather I use the guns they give me."

"And that knife?"

Hogan smiled. "No, they did not give this to me."

Wise Crow held out a hand for the knife, and Hogan handed it over. Studying it carefully, the ancient man felt the edge of the blade lightly, then passed it back.

"It is a fine weapon. A weapon worthy of a chief. Did you buy it?"

Hogan still remembered the occasion when Brom had presented the knife to him.

"No. It was a gift."

"Then you must have become a mighty warrior since last you came to visit many, many moons ago."

"I don't know about 'mighty,' Wise Crow. But I've managed to stay alive."

"Now show me how well you handle the bow."

Hogan found a large cardboard box and drew a crude circle on it with a marking pen. Then he set the box in front of a stack of hay across the sun-dried field from Wise Crow's house.

He stripped off his shirt and stepped down from the porch. Drawing one of the slender sticks from the quiver, he nocked the feathered arrow into the bowstring, then curled his fingers around the waxed gut and pulled it back until the weapon was arched in a deep curve. The muscles in his well-toned body bulged as he sighted down the long, slender length of polished wood.

To anyone studying John Hogan, his holding an archer's bow seemed the most natural act. His long, thin face reflected the brooding features of the Apache Indians who were his mother's people.

He took a deep breath to relax the muscles and make his aim true. Now he was ready to demonstrate to the ancient Apache how he handled the wooden weapon.

Locking his index and middle fingers around the end of the long thin shaft to hold it in position, he raised the bow and aimed it at the paper target.

"You are too determined to hit the target."

The accusation that came from the mouth of Wise Crow sounded familiar, just like the words Mok Seng used at the Cambodian Buddhist temple.

Carefully sighting at the distant target down the line of the long thin shaft, he took a deep breath and released the feathered arrow. With a loud hum from the string, it swiftly flew in an almost straight line and smoothly sliced its way into the edge of the inner circle of the round target.

Wise Crow's voice broke the silence. "A lucky shot," he said impassively.

Hogan looked across the field at the target. The arrow had landed in the center of the hand-drawn circle. He took out another arrow from the bark quiver and let it fly at the target.

Carving through the air, the feathered arrow splintered the first arrow and chewed into the cardboard target.

"Was that one also just luck?"

"You are doing better," Wise Crow said, then disappeared into the house.

Luck held a special meaning for Black Jack. As a counterinsurgent specialist for the United States Army, Hogan had led deep-penetration assaults into the jungles of Southeast Asia, until a surprise attack by Khmer Rouge Communist guerrillas had left him and his squad for dead.

When he'd revived from a nightmare in which he dreamed he had died and got kicked out of hell as a troublemaker, he discovered he was in a small Buddhist temple in northern Cambodia, the only one of his squad to have survived the ambush. Mok Seng had nursed him back to life and proceeded to train his body and mind.

Now Wise Crow emerged from the house carrying a large leather bag. He waved Hogan over to sit on the porch steps.

"This belonged to your father," he said.

Black Jack was surprised. Knowing how much his Scots-descent father and Indian grandfather disliked one another, he was stunned that any of his dead father's belongings were in Wise Crow's possession.

Sitting down, Hogan opened the bag and found a worn leather holster, the .44 Magnum Smith & Wesson revolver his father liked to carry and a dozen hand-loaded cartridges. Carefully checking the barrel, he was surprised to see how clean it was.

"A fine tool deserves fine care," Wise Crow grunted in explanation.

As Hogan loaded six shells into the well-oiled cylinder, he sensed his grandfather studying his face.

"Your body seems fit, but something is troubling your spirit," Wise Crow commented.

Jack Hogan knew that physically he had never been in better shape. Under the daily demands of Mok Seng, he went through a series of exercises designed to maintain the fighting machine his body had become, as well as sharpen his mind and martial arts skills.

Every muscle on his taut six-foot frame was toned to its maximum capacity. His washboard-flat stomach was able to withstand the incessant pounding of an angry opponent, and the edges of his hands were covered with layers of thick calluses created by pounding them against hardwood boards daily.

Only his thoughts were causing him discomfort, as Wise Crow had sensed.

"My friends are being killed one by one. And I don't know why."

Wise Crow picked up a stick and began to whittle. "You have pursued evil for many years. Now it pursues you. It is the way of the blue eyes—your father's people."

In his role as a shaman, Wise Crow usually said things that were based on some inner wisdom or spiritual guidance. But not this time. As much as his grandfather loved him, Hogan knew his comments were generated by his still-existing animosity for the taciturn Scotsman who had convinced his daughter to leave the reservation and marry him, even though both of Black Jack's parents were dead.

Wise Crow's dislike of the settlers who had taken Apache land on which they built their ranches still remained.

Seeing the scowl on Hogan's face, Wise Crow lifted his tired body and pulled himself to his feet. "Come. We will ask the spirits of your ancestors to help find an answer."

Together they walked over to a large structure covered with branches and leaves. A stocky woman guarded the only entrance.

"We will sit in the steam and seek truth in the lodge," he told her.

"The rocks are heated and ready. And there is a pail of cold water inside for the steam. You have an hour," she replied. "Then it will be time for the women to sit among the steaming rocks and meditate."

Shaking his head, Wise Crow led Hogan inside.

The interior of the lodge was dark. Only the flames from a small fire burning in a crudely built fire pit lit the area. Shadows moved along the walls as the two men worked their way to the center of the structure.

"There was a time when only the men would enter the lodge. That is another evil your father's people wished on us. Women who want to be like men. Some have even demanded to do the duty of warriors."

Black Jack smiled. He wondered how the Apache shaman would feel if he were exposed to the Israeli military, where women and men shared the same combat duties. "Times change, Grandfather."

"Too fast." Wise Crow sighed and looked sad. "When I was a young man, only warriors put on war paint. Now only women wear it."

They sat on the blanket spread out on the ground, and Wise Crow opened a small leather pouch he wore on his pants belt. From inside he took out a handful of brightly colored sand and threw it into the fire. A swirl of bright colors bounced up from the fire and fled through the small opening in the roof of the building that allowed smoke to escape.

Mumbling ancient words under his breath, the shaman stared at the fire, then turned his eyes on Hogan. The light from the fire reflected in them, turning Wise Crow's pupils into burning flames.

For close to a half hour, the elderly Indian stared at the fire, ignoring Black Jack, arguing loudly as if there were a third person in the lodge.

Suddenly he reached down to the pail of water at his feet and filled a ladle. Tossing the liquid on the rocks in the fire, he watched the vapors rise and surround him in a cloud of steam.

Hogan felt the presence of something alien. It made him uncomfortable. Instinctively he reached for the large ornate-handled knife he wore at his waistband and waited for his grandfather to speak.

Wise Crow lifted his head and looked at the younger man.

"You have many enemies."

"Most of them are dead," Black Jack replied.

"But not all."

"Who is it?"

A dark, swirling cloud climbed out of the steaming smoke and hovered over Hogan.

"A powerful sorcerer. He comes from another world. Never have I met one like him before. And there are two of you who prevent him from accomplishing what he has come for."

"And what is that, Grandfather?"

"Even the powerful spirits I sent out to learn the answer do not know. But the world we know is in danger." Wise Crow looked unhappy. "You are the last of my blood. Yet it is your mission to stop this creature, even if you must give your life to do it."

Hogan looked surprised. "By myself?"

Wise Crow threw some more of the colored sand into the fire, waited for the sparkling colors to escape through the roof opening, then dashed another ladle of water on the hot stones.

Two light-colored columns of steam rose to the roof of the structure, swirling around and surrounding the dark smoke until it was buried inside them.

Wise Crow seemed puzzled. "The spirits say there are two of you, who together can defeat this strange sorcerer."

Hogan understood even though the ancient Apache didn't. There was another like him, but not of the world that Wise Crow knew. It was Brom, the red-bearded warrior who was lord of Kalabria, an ancient, primitive kingdom in another dimension.

The two had become bonded when their spirits left their dying bodies to search for new physical hosts after each had been critically wounded in battle in their own worlds. Returning to life, the spirit of each returned to its own body, but carried with it a part of the other's spirit, linking the two warriors forever.

"I can explain about the other," he started to reply.

Wise Crow held up a hand. "No. This is beyond my understanding. This is between the two of you."

Black Jack wanted to explain that he still didn't understand how he and Brom could come to each other's aid. For a long time he had thought the Kalabrian warrior was only part of his dreams. Then he realized that Brom and he were part of each other's reality.

The elderly shaman started to get to his feet.

Hogan was surprised. Was this the end of the ceremony? He had so many more questions to ask.

"Is this sorcerer killing my friends?"

"I do not think so. I think those he employs are."

"Why?"

Wise Crow stabbed a long, spindly finger at Hogan's chest. "When you find the answer, you will also find the solution."

After a last stern look, he grumbled, "Come. The women will be arriving soon to demand their time in the men's smoke lodge."

Hogan stood up. It was time for him to drive back to Phoenix and catch a flight that would lead him back to the ancient ruins of Angkor Wat and the small Buddhist temple where he lived.

But he knew that the recent events had marked only the beginning, and soon there would be more to come.

In a short while he had hit the road and was lost in his thoughts until he glanced at the side-view mirror. There he saw a faint outline of Brom, leaning forward in a listening pose.

The image disappeared quickly from the reflecting surface, and Hogan wondered just what was going on in Kalabria.

5

There was no way that Captain Durjam could know he was witnessing what was planned to be the total obliteration of Kalabria.

As the commander of the Kalabrian border guard, he watched in frustration the swarm of shabbily dressed men, women and children approach the frontier outpost that marked the end of the kingdom of Tana and the beginning of Kalabria.

Durjam was a warrior, used to battling armed invaders. These invaders carried no weapons. Just themselves and their skimpy belongings.

The light armor he wore made his heavyset body uncomfortable and added to his irritation.

Sergeant Groz, a grizzled veteran of the frontier guard, rode his large gray stallion to his side.

"There must be thousands of people out there," he said, sounding worried. "Do you think they're planning to try to cross into Kalabria?"

"Of course they're going to try," Durjam growled. "Where were you this morning when I warned the men that more pilgrims were headed our way?"

The sergeant kept staring across the border, stunned at the sea of bodies that moved slowly toward them. "I didn't think there would be this many. You said that small groups were crossing into Kalabria."

"Until now." Durjam drummed the fingers of his right hand on the rigid leather saddle while he evaluated the situation.

Then he made a decision.

"Get back to Tella and tell Lord Brom what's happening here. Meantime, I take the men and try to stop these—" he hesitated "—what the hell are they calling themselves?"

"Children of Ost," Groz said.

"Pretty shabbily dressed children of so great a god, if you ask me, Sergeant," Durjam growled.

CAPTAIN DURJAM slowly led his hundred men to the border and waited for the horde to approach them. As the first pilgrims came up to the stone markers that separated Kalabria from its neighboring kingdom, the captain raised a hand in the air.

"Stop," he shouted.

The procession paused at his words.

"You have no permission to enter Kalabria. If you try to cross the border, we will be forced to take measures to stop you."

He turned and signaled his men.

Two dozen mounted bowmen at either end of the wide line of warriors withdrew arrows from their quivers and nocked them into the bowstrings. The rest of the troop withdrew their swords or raised their maces.

"We don't want to hurt anybody," Durjam shouted. "But if we need to, we will use our weapons."

There was an angry rumble from the crowd on the other side of the border. Then the pilgrims moved to either side to allow a tall, gray-bearded man in a blue robe to move past them.

The captain looked surprised as he recognized the man.

"Mondlock," he said, sounding stunned. "What are you doing here?"

"What is your name, Captain?"

"I am Captian Durjam. We met at the feast for Hogan several months ago. Remember?"

The gray-bearded man nodded. "And you know who I am?"

"Of course. Every Kalabrian knows Mondlock the Knower, the right hand and adviser of Lord Brom."

The man in robes looked satisfied.

"Good. Then hear this. As Lord Brom's adviser—and as a priest of Ost—I order you to let these pilgrims pass into Kalabria."

Durjam remembered the orders from Tella, the capital city.

"Lord Brom himself has ordered us to stop the pilgrims from crossing into our country. Do you realize where they plan to go?"

"Yes. To where the great god Ost dwells."

"They head for the Forbidden Region, where only death awaits them."

"No. They go to find Ost. The great god will take care of his children."

The captain held his ground.

"I have my orders, Mondlock, from Lord Brom himself."

"And I have mine, from someone higher than him."

Durjam signaled his men to move slowly forward, their weapons poised for battle.

"Until Lord Brom gives me different orders, no one will enter Kalabria."

For a moment the two stared at one another. Then the gray-bearded man turned to the mass of people behind them.

"Ost awaits us," he shouted. "The prophet has promised us eternal paradise when we meet the great god. Those who die in his cause will live at his side for all time!"

He turned and led the vast army of walkers toward the mounted troopers.

Captain Durjam hesitated until the first wave of pilgrims began to move past him. Then he rose in his saddle and shouted, "Kalabrians, stop them!"

Reluctantly the mounted soldiers swung their weapons, trying to injure rather than kill. But as one wave of pilgrims fell to the grassy plain, a second wave replaced them.

Again and again the troopers swung their maces and slashed with their already-bloodstained swords.

Arrows flew like angry hornets from the bows of the archers, and the wounded dropped, disappearing from sight in that moving mass of bodies.

Nobody screamed in pain as blades or hammers or arrowheads tore at them. Instead, they kept calling out the name of the god they were seeking.

"Ost, I serve you," they shouted as they fell under the blows from the Kalabrian warriors, only to be trampled by the hordes of pilgrims who stepped on them in their journey forward.

Soon the hundred soldiers were completely surrounded by the walkers.

"In the name of Ost, kill them!" Mondlock yelled.

A calm sea of pilgrims tore at the furious Kalabrian soldiers who slashed and hammered in a desperate effort to fight them off. But they were out-
numbered. And one by one they were pulled from
their horses.

The robed pilgrims fell on the soldiers and tore at
their throats and hands, ripping their weapons from
them and turning them on the Kalabrian guards.

The screams of dying warriors filled the frontier as
the gray-bearded man in robes stood to the side and
quietly watched.

Then he turned and walked to a large tent. He lifted
the flap to gain entry, and just before he disappeared
inside, a jagged streak of light outlined his body,
making him look like a mirage.

As HE STARED at the bound man who sat on the floor
of the tent, the blond man in the blue robe reminded
himself that he was facing the one opponent he could
not best—time. There was no way to measure exactly
how much longer the essential energy would last before existence ceased. He needed to accelerate his
search for the glowing rocks.

"You are Mondlock the Knower, a priest of Ost,"
he said.

"Yes, I am Mondlock. Who are you?"

"I have called myself many names. Perhaps the one
you will know best is Nis. But I am known by others
as a prophet."

Mondlock's face darkened. Nis was the name of the magician who had helped the insane priestess, Raikana, attempt to conquer Kalabria and its neighbors. He had vanished after her death.

Some of the other Knowers had claimed that Nis was a great demon who had risen from the bowels of the world to destroy it. Mondlock did not believe it. But he did believe that the creature who called himself Nis was a powerful sorcerer, capable of terrible magic. What he couldn't decide was what the magician wanted from him.

"Where are the glowing rocks?"

Mondlock was puzzled. The only glowing stones he knew of came from the body of Ost within his secret temple built at the beginning of time. "I know of no rocks that glow."

"There are rumors that the temple of this god you worship is filled with such rocks. Where is it?"

The gray-bearded wise man wondered why the sorcerer was so desperate to find Ost's body. He made up his mind that no torture the magician could invent would force him to reveal its location in the Forbidden Region.

"This whole country is a temple to Ost," he replied with cunning naïveté.

Nis studied the face of the bound man, trying to decide whether he was lying.

He had to be, Nis decided. But what if the man was telling the truth?

He began to feel a new emotion building inside. He couldn't identify it. He estimated he had approximately six months left before the energy ran out. What would happen to him if he could find no glowing rocks by then to replenish himself?

A word came to mind. Fear.

Fear? Nis had never experienced the feeling before this. No. Mondlock was lying.

"You are in no position to play games, Mondlock. Already your friends in Kalabria have become your enemies. They saw you order the death of the border guards."

"What they saw was the image of me you projected there."

"But who will tell them?"

"I will," Mondlock said. "You cannot kill me. If you wish to send projections of me, you must keep me alive."

"Your fate will be sealed by Brom and his Kalabrian warriors. Even now, they are furiously searching for you."

Mondlock knew Nis was right. He wondered if he would be allowed to live long enough to defend himself at a trial.

What worried him more than his own future was the figure that stood before him. He could sense that the man had set something in motion, something beyond the ordinary world of birth and death and the regular rhythms of nature.

SERGEANT GROZ had paused at the top of a nearby hill for a moment. He had been tempted to return and help his comrades fight off the suddenly savage pilgrims, then he realized it was more important to carry the news to Lord Brom in the capital city. Would his news be believed when he could hardly believe it himself?

The great man of wisdom, Mondlock the Knower, was a traitor.

He turned his stallion around, kicked at his sides and raced along the hard-packed road leading to Tella.

6

Hogan was rolling at a steady pace along the dirt roads that led to State Highway 69. His flight wasn't leaving for four hours, so he decided to wander through the pine woods and inhale the fragrant memories that reminded him of his youth.

To reach them he had to drive along the edge of the sacred burial grounds. It was in these same grounds, among her ancestors, where his mother was buried.

The pine-studded hilly area was sacred to the Apaches. It was the spot where the spirits of their gods came to escort the dead to a resting place before they began the journey to find a new body who would host them.

None of the ranchers who lived near the reservation would trespass here. Even the tourists who visited Prescott seemed to respect the signs that warned them to keep out of the sacred area.

Only those with Apache blood ventured here. Like Hogan.

He stopped his rented Jeep and stared through the trees at the forbidding-looking hills beyond them. He was tempted to get out and look at the grave of the woman who had borne him.

Then he decided that the only thing remaining of her under the packed earth were her bones. He still remembered the horror of seeing huge stacks of bleached bones of men, women and children left by the genocidal Khmer Rouge Communist forces who had overrun Cambodia in the late 1970s. He had no need to stand over his mother's grave and imagine her bones beneath his booted feet.

Black Jack glanced at the seat beside him. Wise Crow's bow and quiver of metal-tipped arrows were next to him.

"Use them with honor," the elderly Apache had said as he handed them to his grandson as a parting gift. "If we do not meet again in this life, remember I shall be watching that you never disgrace your heritage."

Honor was important to Wise Crow. Hogan understood that, but for him, survival came before honor.

Keeping his windows open, he let the warm breezes work their way through his denim work shirt and dry the perspiration on his chest.

Crowding around him were memories of a gentler time. He had lived on a large ranch twenty miles from here, the son of a dour rancher and an Apache mother who had no other offspring. His only friends were the ranch hands his father hired during roundup time and the children who lived on the reservation where his mother had been raised.

He had no desire to visit the land on which he had been raised. He had sold the property to an anonymous corporation after his parents had died. From what he'd heard, the once-huge ranch had been carved up into building sites for vacation homes.

His childhood had been lonely. The empty hours, between school and homework, were filled with doing chores. His father had taught him how to use a gun, and his mother's people had bestowed on him the capacity to listen to the land, as well as the skills of the weapons of their ancestry—the bow, the spear, the hunting knife.

With trained eyes Hogan found the almost-hidden signs of deer and small animals. Smiling, he remembered how as a child he would track them, solemnly aiming his air gun at them when they were finally cornered. It wasn't until he was in his teens that he actually pulled the trigger on his gun and bagged game.

He closed his eyes and recalled how he had hid in the woods and stared in shock at the still body of the first antlered stag he had killed.

Things were different now. And so was the game.

But now he wasn't shocked by the death of some criminal who confronted him with the ultimate threat. He had grown from child to man and learned the bitter reality that in the world in which he dealt, there were only the hunted and the hunter.

Then a strange premonition washed over him, and a shiver ran down his spine. He opened his eyes and saw a faintly mottled shimmering begin to move around him.

Hogan grabbed the .44 Magnum and the archery supplies, then glanced down at his waistband and made sure the long knife was in its scabbard while he waited for the mist to transport him.

BROM WAS FURIOUS. His body shook from the effort he made to restrain his rage, and his face was dark.

The rage had started with the arrival of Sergeant Groz from the border guard and his report. Minutes after he had started, Brom exploded and reached for the broadsword he kept constantly at his side.

If Mora hadn't stopped him, Brom would have severed the head from the body of the sergeant who dared lie and say that Mondlock was a traitor.

"You speak of Mondlock the Knower, not some ordinary man," he shouted.

Nervously the grizzled officer looked down at the rugs that covered the throne room. "If I hadn't seen him with my own eyes, Lord Brom, I would have slain anyone who would have dared to accuse Mondlock of murdering Kalabrian soldiers," he mumbled.

The flaxen-haired woman who sat at the red-bearded leader's side leaned over. "He speaks the truth," she said in a low voice.

Brom turned his head and looked at her with icy eyes.

"Even you believe this of Mondlock?"

"The sergeant only tells what he saw. Perhaps it was some evil magic that forced the Knower into his actions."

The chieftain rose from the huge carved throne that had been built for one of his ancestors. He hated sitting in the massive chair. His place was atop a well-trained stallion leading his men into battle, and not inside a stuffy room making political decisions.

Pacing the large room, he kept glancing at Mora, then at the sergeant. Finally he made his decision.

"You will lead me and my personal guard to the spot where you saw Mondlock commit this hideous act. And if it turns out you have lied, you will die many deaths before you stop living."

7

Sitting behind his large desk in the basement of the United Nations headquarters complex on New York City's First Avenue, Jaako Rinmann, aide to the secretary general, stared at the message that had been left on his desk in the middle of the night.

His visitor watched the expression on Rinmann's face turn to horror.

"Is something wrong?"

Rinmann forced himself to break the hypnotic spell the message had created and looked at the sandy-haired man sitting across the desk from him.

Llewellyn Hazelford had returned a few weeks ago from heading up the peacekeeping troops in Lebanon. He was helping out with odd jobs at the UN while he waited for reassignment.

Rinmann handed the message to him. The retired British officer read it aloud.

"The use of nuclear power is destroying our planet. We demand that use of nuclear energy be stopped immediately. We have tried through peaceful means to achieve this, but we were ignored. Therefore, within seventy-two hours, any nuclear facility still functioning and occupied will be destroyed, then we will take over all uncooperative governments. This is not an idle threat as you will learn today."

The paper was signed, "The Council of Anti-Nuclear Organizations."

"Sounds as though they meant it," Hazelford commented.

"I think so," Rinmann agreed in a stricken voice.

In the twenty years he had been in diplomacy—first as a member of the Swedish delegation and now as part of the United Nations administration—Jaako Rinmann had been witness to threats from terrorist groups. The Japanese Red Army, the Baader Meinhof gang, even the Irish Republican Army had all attempted to use the international organization as a way of making their demands known to the world.

But never before had any group threatened to take control of the entire world.

There was no point wondering how the letter found its way through the UN security guards to his office. There was always someone—a cleaning person, a clerk or a junior member of one of the delegations—who would handle such an assignment for a fee.

Suddenly he jumped to his feet. "I have to show this to the secretary general," he exclaimed, and moved quickly to the door.

Llewellyn Hazelford waited until the frightened man left his office, then took out his pipe and carefully filled it with pungent tobacco from a leather pouch. Seeming completely at ease, he started the task of getting his pipe going.

He wondered how Rinmann would react if he knew that the very same person who placed the message on his desk had just read it aloud minutes ago.

He'd find out soon enough. After the group's plans were carried out.

And Jennifer and the two girls would rest a little easier in their graves for what he had done this day to avenge the criminal actions that had taken their lives. He had been commanding British troops in Belfast, trying to keep the Catholics and Protestants from destroying each other.

One night IRA killers had planted a bomb in the family car. The next morning the Hazelford family was dead, with the exception of the general. All because a weak-spined British government refused to follow his suggestion that the only way to handle the IRA was to line up every suspect and their families and shoot them.

As he thought about it again, he agreed with the American general. It would be a better world after they took over.

8

As Hogan looked around at the familiar landscape, he realized that the shimmering cloud had transported him to the primitive land called Kalabria.

He recognized the grassy plains and gentle rolling hills, surrounded by high mountains to the east, west and north. To the south, the plains and hills ran into the horizon.

First the neon green grassy plains, broken by patches of wooded areas, stretched for countless miles to the range of cobalt blue mountains in the distance. He could barely make out the dense forests that separated the tall grass country from the towering peaks.

Overhead, a cloudless lavender-tinted sky glowed down on a wide angry river of icy yellow water slashing the land into two roughly equal halves. Large glittering rocks jutted up from the riverbed and tried, unsuccessfully, to interrupt the rapid flow of frothing water.

He looked up at the sky. Even in the heat of day, he could make out the faint outlines of the twin moons that moved in a predetermined path around this world.

Somewhere nearby, Brom needed his help. But where? All around him the undulating land looked peaceful and quiet.

Hogan turned his attention to the wide packed-dirt road that traversed the plains and led to a low bridge of rough-hewn planks spanning the river. It was the only link Hogan could see that connected the two halves of land.

For an hour he walked past untouched fields of razor grass and thorn brush, with sweat trickling down his face. Hogan paused to rest, thinking how sweet the water from a swift stream would taste at the moment.

A small twisted tree offered a small shaded square of brambly grass beneath its sickly branches. Hogan eased his body under it and gingerly let his head rest against the unfamiliar ground.

Ten minutes of dozing. That's all he'd take before he continued on his journey. He let his lids close out the sun from his eyes when a familiar sound reached his ear.

He opened his eyes and sat up.

A riderless horse—a massive, chestnut-colored animal with a mane of black—was charging toward him. The horse stared at him with large fiery eyes, then turned its head away and continued its panicked flight.

Hogan dropped his rifle and jumped to his feet, then cupped his mouth and made a low braying sound. The startled animal stopped and turned its head toward the source of the noise.

Hogan raced toward it and grabbed the loose reins. The animal concentrated its fury in its powerful neck, twisting and turning to be free.

Hogan allowed the angry animal to drag him on his heels until he could grab a handful of mane. Then swiftly he pulled himself up into the wooden saddle mounted on the back of the terrified animal.

While Hogan dug his heels into the sides of his mount, the furious creature bucked and tried to throw him from its back. Running, bucking, twisting, braying, snorting its ire, the animal continued to try to unseat the man on its back.

Hogan hung on as though he had become one with the horse. He could make out the distant sounds of battle now, and it would be a long hot walk without a mount beneath him.

Suddenly the creature stopped the contest and surrendered. Standing calmly, the horse turned its head and looked back.

Hogan spoke quietly to it for a long time, petting it as he did, then slid from the saddle and retrieved his rifle.

Pulling himself back onto the chestnut, he set off.

Man and horse rode steadily, passing a village and several huts along the road. It was only when he started getting thirsty that he realized he had not seen another person since he had started.

He kept looking for a stream or brook as he continued his journey toward the sounds. Without success.

The huts disappeared as he passed along the edge of a thickly wooded area. The low-hanging trees provided temporary relief from the heat of the midday sun.

Watching carefully for hidden attackers, Hogan spurred his mount past the forest. Ahead of him was another small village of thatched-roof huts. Hogan searched for signs of life. Nothing. Not even an animal. As in the other village, life had vanished.

Neat stacks of drying plains grass were lined up along the road. Hogan could feel his lips start to crack from lack of moisture. Beneath him the angry stallion had lost much of its fire and was trembling, covered with froth at the mouth.

"It's time we found ourselves some water and a place to rest," he said, his voice sounding like metal rubbed against a rasp.

Hogan reined in the mount and walked him gingerly through the fields until he came to a large thatched-roof structure.

It looked like a barn. A perfect place to rest from the sun. He dismounted the chestnut-colored animal and wrapped the reins around a wooden railing.

There was a stone well nearby. Hogan walked to it and found a wooden bucket on the ground. A crude hand-pulled hoist sat on a wooden frame mounted atop the well.

He attached the bucket to the end of a rope and lowered it until he heard the soft splash, then jiggled the rope until the pull of the rope signaled the bucket was full. Slowly he pulled up the bucket.

He could almost taste the cool water running down his parched throat as he untied the bucket. Lifting the wooden pail to his lips, he started to drink when he heard the soft rustling sound behind him.

Turning quickly, he saw the rusted tines of a pitchfork rushing at him. Swiftly he moved to one side and grabbed the wooden handle. With a powerful jerk, he tore the weapon from the hands of his attacker.

It was then that he saw the frightened small girl who had fallen to the ground. She was thin, wearing rags, and her light brown hair fell across her face in a tangled heap.

Hogan glanced at her feet. They were bare. The child of farmers.

Hogan gave her a reproving look. "Is it a crime to want a drink?"

"I thought you were one of the men who forced my father and mother to go with them." She got to her feet and nervously moved away.

Hogan put the bucket down on the ground and gestured for the girl to come to him. She shook her head and continued to back away.

"Do I look like any of the men who were here before?"

"No," she admitted with an edge of caution in her voice. "They wore robes."

"What kind of robes?"

"Just like some of our priests'."

"Did you recognize the men who took your parents away?"

"No. They told us a prophet had ordered that we join the pilgrims and help search for the god Ost. My parents didn't want to go, but they forced them at sword point. I ran and hid under the dried grass so they wouldn't find me."

There was something special about the child. Despite her fear, Hogan could sense a defiance in her.

He smiled at her encouragingly. "What is your name?"

"Simma," she said.

"You can't stay here alone, Simma. Not even to care for the farm animals until your parents return. It isn't safe."

"There are no animals. The robed men took them with them."

"Do you have any other family?"

The young girl shook her head.

Hogan remembered the thousands of homeless Cambodian children who had been left to sell themselves on the streets for enough money to buy food. Surely someone would take the child.

"You will come with me."

At first the young girl looked around as if she was about to bolt. Then she studied Hogan's expression. Something in it seemed to reassure her that he meant no harm.

She nodded, then suddenly turned and ran into the barn. Hogan started to follow, when the child came out dragging a large sack. Handing it up to Hogan, she said, "There is bread and strips of meat. Dry and hard, but not spoiled." She sounded proud as she added, with a smile, "I prepared them myself."

The smile on Simma's face vanished as she stared past Hogan in terror. "They're back," she shouted, running to where the pitchfork still lay on the ground.

Hogan twisted in his saddle. Two men had crawled through the tall grass behind him. The first of the pair rushed forward and whirled his long sword in a wide arc. Hogan's first instinct was to use his father's revolver, then he remembered he only had a dozen cartridges.

Instead, he pulled the bow from his shoulder, whipped a metal-tipped arrow from the bark case and pulled back on the bowstring until it was bent into a deep arc.

He let his mind go calm, then released the bow. The feather-edged shaft tore into the throat of the nearest of the two and released a fountain of blood.

Clenching a short, studded mace, the second man charged. Hogan jumped from the saddle and grabbed the three-foot-long blade from the now-still hand of the first attacker. He could feel the weight and delicate balance that made this a fine weapon.

"Come meet your death," he shouted as he rushed at the surprised opponent.

From a corner of his eye, Black Jack saw Simma rushing at the robed man with the pitchfork. Before he could stop her, he saw the remaining assailant trying to decide whom he would fight first.

And that was his last mistake.

Hogan raised the huge sword with both hands and carved a wide path down his opponent's body. The swish of the sword through the air was a death sentence, and the attacker became a disjointed, bloodied heap.

Hogan turned and saw Simma standing frozen, pitchfork still clenched in her hands, staring in horror at the carnage. There was no way to explain what he had done, or why.

"You will understand when you are older," he said, and turned away from her shocked face. "Don't look anymore—rest your eyes on the fields. Time will heal this hideous vision."

9

She stopped and glanced at the summer fashions displayed in the little shop's window. But Valerie Wilding didn't care about the clothes on display. She wanted to see if the same two men were with her.

In the reflection of the glass, she saw them. Leaning against a parked car, the two were neatly dressed in sports clothes. She didn't know what they had in mind, but these weren't the run-of-the-mill hoodlums shown on television shows. These two were professionals.

She recognized the type. Despite their conservative outfits, their expressions gave them away. Or rather, lack of expressions.

The problem was she didn't know why they were tailing her.

For several days she had felt that she was being followed.

So Valerie decided to take no chances. She made sure that every minute of her day was filled with appointments with groups of people.

Her nights were spent away from her small Georgetown apartment. Usually with a different man each time. And finding men was not a problem for Valerie. She was tall, shapely, and exuded a raw sensuality. There were two reasons for it.

The first was self-preservation. The second was to get even with Jim Holaday for ignoring her the past several months.

She kept calling in from outside telephones and checking her answering machine. He still hadn't returned her calls, and she was tempted to try calling him one more time. To ask him what she should do about the two men.

But she knew the reason she didn't. She suspected they had been sent by Jim.

Maybe he was worried that she would tell somebody about his business arrangement with the Laotian warlord. Many times he had reminded her that most of the money she used to live on came from Soong's business, not from the retirement she received as an air force major. Jim had warned her regularly about keeping her mouth shut.

She knew better than he did how good the business was. While he played the role of the retired hero to the hilt, she and Becker were busy running things.

But even though she had resented it, she knew why he constantly lectured her. She liked a few drinks now and then. And when she got drunk, she liked to brag.

It hadn't always been that way. Just since she joined Soong's organization. Every time she read a story about a teenager dying from an overdose of narcotics, she could feel the guilt tearing at her.

Even Jim's reassurances hadn't helped. "Look at it this way, Val," he would tell her. "Soong's customers are the non-whites, not decent American Christians."

Both of them knew he was lying—or at least she hoped he knew.

No, even though Jim worried about her drinking, she was certain he realized she was smart enough not to reveal information about Soong's operation and send herself to jail.

It had to be something else, and she flipped through her memory for a clue. But nothing came to mind. Unless . . .

She wondered if it had anything to do with the strange man with whom they'd had dinner several months ago. He called himself Father Vigilante although he explained he wasn't an ordained priest, but what he talked about was war, not peace.

Jim Holaday had been intrigued and flattered that the millionaire with perfect, unmarked face, yellow hair and almond-shaped eyes had sought him out.

They'd talked about the confusion in the world, now that the strong government controls had been loosened in so many countries to give people a more direct voice in the operation of their countries.

They had gotten into heated discussions about a possible solution when Jim had stopped and insisted on sending her home in a cab.

He had begun to pull away from her that night. He had returned to her apartment just before dawn, claiming he had to leave for his ranch immediately.

That was the last time she had seen or spoken to him. But if the men following her had been sent by Jim, she didn't want to find out what they had in mind.

As she kept pretending to study the new fashions, she made a decision. She was going to disappear.

STANDING NEXT to the orphaned Kalabrian child, Hogan looked out at the road. A long parade of people were moving aimlessly along it. For a moment he thought they were allies of the two dead men, then he studied the weary, hopeless expressions on their faces and changed his mind.

He called out to them. "Where are you bound?"

Terrified, a handful of elderly men froze and stared at him.

Then one of them looked at the two bodies and relaxed. He turned to the others.

"It's all right. He is not one of those who drive the pilgrims," he said loudly.

As Black Jack remembered, Brom had mentioned the problems with pilgrims.

He stared at the man who had spoken and asked, "Who are you?"

"I am called Beshar. I—" he turned and waved to the long line of weary travelers "—we are from Tana."

Hogan had heard of Tana. It was Kalabria's nearest neighbor.

"Why are you here in Kalabria?"

For a moment the man who called himself Beshar shivered with fear. "We were forced to come here by the soldiers of the so-called prophet. We have run away from them."

"Why? Who are these pilgrims?"

"A group of robed men who called themselves 'the children of Ost' came to us a month ago with a message from the prophet of Ost. If the Tanians would acknowledge that Ost was the supreme god, they would be spared when the end of the world came.

"We are a faithful people, so of course we agreed. Then the messengers added one more condition. Every Tanian must join in the pilgrimage to find Ost in the Forbidden Region. Those who did not would be immediately punished by Ost.

"Because it was nearly the harvest season, Lazak, our head Knower, explained we would have no food for ourselves or our animals if we deserted our farms now. Lazak asked if he could speak to the prophet on our behalf. They led him away to a large, black tent from which emerged a young blond man with strange eyes who led him inside."

Hogan's eyes narrowed, and he gestured for the elderly man to continue.

"Several hours later Lazak came out of the tent and returned to us. He had a strange, empty look in his eyes. But we assumed it was exhaustion from whatever ordeal he had been put through."

Another of the Tanian leaders picked up the story at that point. "We talked to him. He said it hadn't been so terrible. He'd only had to listen to words from the blond man and join him in prayers to Ost. But we had to all follow the prophet immediately."

"His woman, Hoka, and his two young children rushed to him, joyous that he was unharmed. As the others watched in horror, Lazak choked Hoka until she died at his feet, then pulled out the long knife he wore in his belt and killed first his children, then himself.

"The creature who called himself a prophet announced that Ost had come and personally punished Lazak and his family. That the same would happen to each of us if we disobeyed the will of Ost. So we gathered up our families and pretended to follow the others until we could slip away in the night."

"Why do you plan to go?"

"We are certain Lord Brom will give us sanctuary," Beshar said.

"Yes. I am sure he will." Hogan pointed to the road he had traveled. "Make your way to Tella—the road is well marked—and tell the guards that Hogan has sent you."

A series of whispered comments quickly passed through the long line of refugees.

"We have heard of Hogan, who is Brom's friend," Beshar said as he started to kneel.

Black Jack stopped him, then turned and beckoned Simma to his side.

"The price for my help is that you take this child—her name is Simma—with you to the city of Tella. Go to the palace of Brom and ask for a woman named Astrah. Tell her I send this child to her for safekeeping."

"It shall be done," Beshar promised.

Hogan studied the face of the small girl, then without knowing why, scooped her up into his huge arms and hugged her.

"You will be safe with Astrah. Tell her I will come to see her—and you—soon," he said in a low voice. Then he tousled Simma's thick thatch of brown hair and winked.

For the first time since they met, the child smiled.

Hogan handed her to the leader of the Tanian refugees.

Beshar took the child and studied the American. "I have heard it said that Hogan was sent by the gods themselves to fight evil. Is it true?"

Black Jack shook his head. "The gods do not share their plans with me." He looked at the man who called himself Beshar. "Lord Brom. Have you seen him?"

Beshar looked blank. But somebody else—a short, weary-looking man—stepped out in front of him.

"My family and I were able to escape the camp of the prophet before dawn. In the hills—" he turned and pointed to a series of small rises in the near distance "—we saw campfires. I heard some say they belonged to the Kalabrian soldiers."

Hogan nodded and as he turned away, something caught his eye. A reflection of sunlight in the pail of water he had set down. The American looked down at it and saw Brom's vague, watery image trembling on the surface of the water.

Jumping into the saddle, he wheeled his steed in the direction of the hills and raced toward them.

A SLIGHT FIGURE sat cross-legged in front of the giant Buddha covered with gold leaf and let his mind open up to the spiritual vibrations filling the large room.

Hidden in the ruins of the ancient city of Angkor Wat, the temple had witnessed over a thousand years of history pass its thick stone walls. Kings and Communists had fought bloody battles on the roads and fields surrounding it. War elephants that once had carried fierce soldiers gave way to metal beasts that depended on gasoline and oil instead of grass to keep them going.

But nothing like the American had come inside its walls. Hogan was different. From a virtually dead soldier, the powerful man had become a warrior of legend.

Something had happened to the American during that period from when his monks had brought the still body to Mok Seng and the hollow-eyed American opened his shut lids and looked up at him.

The abbot had seen much that could not be explained in human terms during his seventy years of life. But nothing like the images Hogan shared with him of the strange, primitive world existing in another time and dimension. And of a red-bearded warrior with whom he had become linked.

These were not the ravings of a man who had lost all sense of reality. At times Mok Seng could feel the reality of the other world, and within it, that small country Hogan called Kalabria.

And when the American, who had become like a son to him, vanished from time to time, Mok Seng knew he had been summoned to that other world.

That was where he had to be now. And all Mok Seng could do was ask the Buddha to watch over him, as any father would ask for a son.

"Guide him, Buddha," the tiny monk said softly, "and lead him along the right path back to here that he may use his strength to protect his own world from the evil threatening it."

Mok Seng did not know what the evil was. All he knew was that it was here and could destroy the world if Hogan did not return and fight it.

FROM THE TOP OF THE HILL Brom could hear the chanting of the wanderers—"the children of Ost" they called themselves—from over the hills. They sat around countless campfires, men, women and children, sharing what little food they had carried with them.

This was like no battle he had ever fought. He did not look forward to the morning, when he would lead his troops and order the shabbily dressed hordes to leave Kalabria.

Dying didn't frighten him. He had already faced the keeper of the underworld in his dreams and spit in his face.

But he had no stomach for driving unarmed pilgrims from his land. According to the scouts who had crawled to the top of the hills to observe them, the nomads kept mumbling prayers to Ost—the great god who had fathered the family of gods and had created the universe. It seemed as though they expected him to descend from his home in the mountains high above the vast desert—called the Forbidden Region—at whose edge they were camped and lead them to some paradise.

He shook a giant fist at the hills in frustration. He was still furious that Mondlock the Knower had been accused of being a traitor and a murderer. But the man who did the accusing was a loyal officer and not given to hallucinations.

If Mondlock had been present, Brom was sure he would have had some reasonable explanation for his behavior and he could convince the pilgrims that they faced hideous perils.

Only a fool or death-seeker would wander into the Forbidden Region without the protection of Ost. Not even Brom would needlessly face the flame-throwing dragons who hid behind the huge boulders, waiting for unsuspecting travelers to pass by before they revealed themselves and consumed their prey with fire from their nostrils.

As he stood proud and erect on the hill, the Lord of Kalabria seemed unafraid of man or demon. His bright red hair and full beard that seemed to glow, his nose, showing the marks of countless encounters with fists and metal, and his eyes, dark and piercing, like those of a cobra seeking the opportunity to strike, all proclaimed the same warning: "Fight me and die!"

He had been born to rule, but ruling was not what he preferred. Brom was a battler, an adventurer who relished challenge and the sound of his howling sword as it clashed against the steel weapon of an enemy.

He left the daily tasks of politics to Mondlock and spent his time preparing himself and his men for the next battle.

He turned and looked at the camp in the valley below. A hundred trained warriors sat around small campfires, grumbling at the unpleasant task awaiting them in the morning.

Brom had no more taste for the job than his men.

One of his captains, a grizzled veteran of many wars named Lodar, lumbered up to his side. "I have posted guards on the hills to keep an eye on the intruders as you ordered, Lord Brom."

"Good. I don't want them slipping away into the Forbidden Region while we are sleeping."

Lodar looked up at the sky. The twin moons were overhead and particularly bright. "Jupo and his sister Lusa watch over us with their light."

He hesitated before asking, "Will Hogan join us in our campaign?"

Brom shook his head. "I don't think we need the help of the great warrior." He slapped the veteran soldier on the back. "Get some rest. We all will need our strength tomorrow."

The captain slapped his breast armor in salute and walked away in the direction of the campfires.

Brom waited until he was alone before looking up at the sky.

"Hogan, I wish you were here. I have never faced anything like this before. And Mondlock is not here to advise me."

Suddenly he heard a voice raised from the camp of the pilgrims.

"Ost has brought us here to serve him. When the sun reaches the center of the sky, gather up your belongings and your families and cross into the desert. There you will find the great god among the sands. Bring me each glowing rock that we may put the bits of Ost together and have him speak to us."

Brom straightened his eyes and tried to penetrate the dark. He could not see the speaker. All he saw was a tall thin figure in a robe around whom the others were gathered.

There was something strange about the speaker, and at the same time something familiar. If only Mondlock were here. He would know who the speaker was. Mondlock knew everything.

For a moment Brom was tempted to mount his horse and charge into the pilgrims' camp to confront the speaker, but he shook his head. He couldn't accomplish anything that way.

He heard a rustling behind him. Turning quickly, he saw the three crouching figures dressed as Kalabrian soldiers hiding in the stretch of high grass below him. He recognized one of them. It was Lodar.

Even as he started to ask why he had come back, Brom saw a too-familiar expression in his eyes. The look of the fanatic. And the short, wide sword in his hand.

Somehow the leader of the pilgrims had converted him into one of his own.

As Lodar growled and charged at him, Brom ripped the long knife from its scabbard and slashed at the crazed officer's fighting arm, carving a deep bloody groove in his wrist.

The other two men, disguised as Kalabrian soldiers, flashed huge axes as they threw themselves into the battle.

There was no time to reach for the howling sword strapped to his back, Brom decided. He'd have to make do with his wits and the krall in his hands.

The wounded officer shouted an incoherent curse as he tried to ram his weapon into Brom's chest.

Brom jumped back, then spun around and skewered the rogue captain's belly with the point of his long knife. Stooping down, he snatched the short sword from the dying man's hand just as a battle-ax carved the empty air inches above his head.

Throwing himself into a forward roll, Brom landed between the legs of one of the two remaining assassins. Without hesitation, he struck upward, and the dying assailant shrieked before he fell forward.

Brom tried to free the embedded weapon from the body, then looked up and saw the battle-ax rising above him.

The victorious grin of the last attacker changed into one of pain as he dropped the ax and grabbed for his neck. Brom could see blood suddenly pouring out of a severed artery as the man gagged on his own blood and slumped to the grass.

The red-haired warrior raised his eyes and saw the piercing stare of the warrior who was his twin from another dimension. He was holding the knife Brom had given him as a gift in one hand and a long sword glistening with blood in the other.

"Next time I wish you could give me a little advance warning so I could carry more suitable weapons," Hogan said calmly.

"You did fine with what you are holding," Brom replied heartily. "I'm glad you arrived when you did."

"You knew I'd be here."

The Kalabrian nodded. They would always be there for each other. It was their lifelong bond.

Hogan looked around. "What's going on?"

"The pilgrims I spoke of," Brom said, pointing toward the huge gathering below them.

"Too bad Mondlock isn't here."

"Just as well," Brom replied, and quickly related the news about Mondlock.

Hogan whistled. "You believe that?"

"No. It's as if someone had cast an evil spell over the whole world."

Black Jack told his own story about the attack by the two mercenaries and his conversation with the peasants from Tana.

"This prophet must be a powerful sorcerer," Brom decided. "And evil."

"I'd say he was one nasty son of a bitch." Hogan rested his hands on his saddle. "What do you want to do about it?"

The Kalabrian leader studied the angry expression on Hogan's face. Then Brom's eyes were suddenly filled with the glint of excitement at the pending battle. "The same as you wish to do."

"Then let's get your men and kick ass."

Brom paused and looked confused.

Hogan grinned. "What I mean is that we will send this prophet creep back to wherever he came from."

SLOWLY Brom and Hogan led a hundred armored and mounted warriors into the camp of the pilgrims. A wide array of weapons were ready to be used at the first sign of resistance.

Longbows were fitted with barbed arrows and arched. Broadswords and maces were raised, ready to cut down any who tried to stop them.

The crowd parted with a murmur to open up paths for the horses. All of them led to the gathering of tents.

Brom raised his hand and signaled his troops to stop. He turned to a frightened-looking young mother who carried an infant in her arms.

Brom and Hogan exchanged glances. Was she a willing pilgrim or was she simply too afraid to leave the encampment?

The red-haired leader moved to the side of the road and reached out his huge arms. Scooping the startled woman and her child onto his saddle, Brom tried to comfort her with his words.

"Where is your man?"

She looked around, then spoke quietly. "They killed him, Lord Brom."

The Kalabrian showed his surprise. "You know me?"

"You came on an official visit to Tana." Her voice cracked, on the verge of tears. "My husband was one of the guardsmen at the palace."

"Then why are you here?"

"They threatened to kill my baby if I didn't come along."

The red-haired commander had thought enough about death for one day. He wanted to think about life. "What is your baby's name?"

"Litina." She blushed. "My husband used to call her Liti when we were alone," she added shyly.

Brom took the infant from her and held it high in the air.

"Liti has withdrawn from the pilgrimage," he shouted. "So has her mother. And so can any of you who wish to do so."

For ten minutes no one moved. Then a young man, swathed in bandages, walked up to the Kalabrian leader's horse.

"I wish to withdraw and leave with you, Lord Brom."

The red-beard pointed to the young woman. "Lead her and her baby to a safe place behind my troops."

"Liti is a seemly name for so tiny a girl," Brom commented, then turned to the young man. "Take good care of both of them," he said sternly. Steadfastly he refused to look at Hogan.

But Hogan only grinned. He knew the red-bearded leader hated displaying tenderness.

Then he noticed that cold-featured men in robes were quietly pushing the other pilgrims back and taking their places. Slowly several hundred men had formed a series of human walls between Hogan and the Kalabrians and the tent where their prophet supposedly was.

He leaned over and pointed to the rapidly forming battle groups.

"I have noticed," Brom murmured back.

Hogan loosened the .44 in its holster. He'd save the handful of shells he had as a last resort. The long sword he had acquired was sheathed in its scabbard on the side of his saddle, ready for Black Jack to free it.

He wrapped his large hand around the sword handle and saw Brom do the same.

"Ready?"

Brom looked around at his men, appraisingly. "All of us are, Hogan."

"This is where the shit hits the fan," Black Jack cracked, then remembered that Brom had never heard the expression.

But Brom wasn't paying attention. He tore his giant broadsword from its shoulder support, waving it over his head until it howled in the wind it created, and turned back to his captains. "Break into three groups." Turning to the one beside him, he ordered,

"You follow us down the middle. And you two, take the right and left flanks."

Brom raised his voice. "Die like warriors!" he shouted. "And take ten of this false prophet's cowards to the underworld with you!"

Then Brom spurred his horse forward. Next to him, Hogan loosened the reins he gripped. Sensing the forthcoming fight, the chestnut stallion reared its head and charged.

The front line of men who guarded the ground between the Kalabrians and the tent let their robes fall and revealed their weapons. Short swords, favored by foot soldiers, battle-axes and maces flashed in their hands. Behind them were men with short bows fitted with metal-barbed arrows and fishhook lances.

The Kalabrian troops were similarly armed.

The two forces mingled with a clashing of steel, while the battle became a series of individual duels. All around Black Jack, steel clanged on steel. Beside him, a young Kalabrian was felled, and Hogan brought his sword into play. With a single stroke Hogan cut the warrior's killer down.

Brom charged into the fight, slashing his huge sword from left to right, driving the enemy before him. Bellowing with the rage of combat, he disregarded his own safety to come to the rescue when his men were at sword point.

The cry of the wounded filled the air, and the flashing of weapons was followed by bright spurts of blood.

Hogan thrust one of the enemy away from himself, but another man rushed him from the left. His horse danced away, but Hogan leaned out of the saddle to deliver a death blow to the head. He looked around for Brom and saw that an attacker had maneuvered himself right behind the Kalabrian leader, who was engaged in a ringing sword fight.

Shoving the sword in the saddle scabbard, Hogan grabbed his bow. He quickly nocked a barb-tipped arrow in the string and let the shaft fly at the assassin.

The man grunted as his lungs were pierced and let his mace fall to the ground. With a great last effort he said, "The prophet will win in the end." Then he tumbled to the ground.

Suddenly the sky became dark, and the flaps of the large tent opened. A hooded figure stepped outside and raised his hands.

"Now feel the wrath of the prophet of Ost," a clear and resonant voice shouted loudly.

A wall of invisible energy, far greater than anything those on the field had ever experienced, slammed into the battlers—friend and foe—lifting them into the air, then throwing them to the ground.

Brom and Hogan were thrown off their horses, then slammed against the ground. Momentarily stunned, the two warriors pulled themselves up into sitting positions and looked around.

What had been, only moments earlier, the site of a great battle was now a funeral ground. Broken bodies covered the field. Soldiers of both sides were piled on one anther, twisted from the violence of the sudden invisible storm.

Brom and Hogan stared at each other, their faces filled with confusion, then looked beyond the battleground.

The whole great crowd of pilgrims, consisting of families with their young, lay still, like a giant mound of broken and useless debris.

The prophet had spared none, and neither Brom nor Hogan knew how they had managed to stay alive.

Staggering to his feet, Hogan moved over to Brom's side.

"Let's see how this 'prophet' deals with cold steel," he said bitterly.

Together they moved to the tent, pausing only for a second before they pushed their way inside.

They stopped in their tracks. Mondlock the Knower stood motionless in the middle of the tent as though he were a statue. Then he lifted his hand accusingly. "You were warned to let the prophet of Ost and his pilgrims pass peacefully," he said in a hollow voice. "The deaths outside this tent are your doing."

Brom seemed shocked. This was the man who had become like a father to him after his own parents had been assassinated. Now he had just admitted he was a traitor—and a murderer.

A wave of sadness washed through him, and as though seeking advice, he looked at Hogan.

But something didn't seem right to Black Jack Hogan. He had met the wise man before, and nothing about the way he spoke or behaved seemed right.

Suddenly it didn't matter. This man had murdered hundreds of soldiers and civilians.

Hogan pulled out his .44 Magnum that had belonged to his father and emptied the six cartridges at the gray-bearded man before Brom could stop him.

Mondlock crumpled beneath his huge robes as he fell to the floor of the tent.

"You have killed Mondlock!" Brom said in rage, raising his huge broadsword threateningly.

By then Hogan had moved to where Mondlock had fallen. Kneeling, he lifted the heavy garments and stared at the ground.

There was no one there. Mondlock had vanished.

"Mondlock has resorted to sorcery," Brom said in shock.

"Or he was never here," Hogan replied.

"But we saw him."

"We saw his image. An old magician's trick where I come from."

"But where did Mondlock go?"

"Probably he was never here." Hogan saw the puzzled look on Brom's face. "Don't ask me how it was done. I don't know. All I know is that this so-called prophet knows a lot of nasty tricks."

"What do we do now?" Brom asked, bewildered.

Hogan glanced at him and saw the blood flowing freely from slashes in his arm and side.

"Get you bandaged up."

Brom managed a smile. "You must have taken a few blows yourself," he said, staring at Hogan.

"Me?" Hogan was surprised to see his entire left side covered with blood. "I never even knew I had been wounded."

He didn't hear the Kalabrian's reply because a great wave of darkness washed over him, but mixed in with it was a golden shimmering tide.

10

Becker knocked on the door to the general's office, then opened the door and went in. Holaday looked up from the papers on his desk.

"I've arranged for another team to take care of Jack Hogan," Becker said.

Holaday nodded and went back to the papers. A moment later he realized he wasn't alone yet.

"Anything else?"

Becker hesitated. "The two men I hired in Washington just called. Valerie Wilding has disappeared," he added apologetically.

Holaday slammed his hand on the desk. "Then have them find her. She's liable to contact the authorities just to get back at me."

Becker, hard faced, waited for Holaday to calm down.

"I don't think so. She's as involved as the rest of us."

"I'm not talking about Soong's business," Holaday growled angrily.

"There isn't much she can tell them."

"More than you think. She knows the names of the others involved and the targets we discussed—even if she doesn't know the full details. It's enough."

Becker understood. Privately he had wondered why the general had pushed her out of his life. With his assistance, she had run the day-to-day operations of the distributing business.

"Who do you think she would contact?"

Holaday shook his head. "I don't know. The FBI. The Pentagon. The CIA..." He paused. "The CIA. There was an agent we worked with who was head-quartered in Bangkok." He leaned back and closed his eyes. "Williams? No, not Williams." He stared at the photographs on the far wall.

There was one of him with Valerie and another man. A short, stout man, impeccably dressed.

"Wilson. Hiram Wilson. That was his name. If she contacts anybody, it will be him."

"Is he still with the CIA?"

"I haven't spoken to him in ten years. But the CIA types never really retire."

"If I can find him, I can make certain she doesn't get to him."

"Or that nobody can get to him," Holaday replied coldly, then added, "If you get my meaning."

"I get it, General."

VALERIE WILDING was terrified as she peeked from behind the lowered blinds of her second floor Holiday Inn motel room. The dark sedan was still there with the two men who had been following her for the past twenty-four hours.

She had driven a circuitous route to the outskirts of Baltimore, checking through her rearview mirror to make sure she hadn't been followed. They must have been better than she thought. Only a professional would have known how to tail her without being spotted.

She had been searching her memory for a reason someone would have hired them ever since she first realized she was being watched. It still came down to Jim Holaday or the Laotian. She had tried to call Jim to reassure him she had no intention of contacting the Drug Enforcement Administration, no matter how she felt about him personally. There was no other explanation for the presence of the hit men—because that was what they looked like.

She wondered why they hadn't attempted to come up and get her, then she glanced at the driveway and saw the reason. A couple of Maryland state troopers were sitting in their official car chatting with some cleaning women in front of the Holiday Inn.

The brunette let the edge of the blind go and picked up a lit cigarette from the ashtray. She looked at her hand. It was shaking.

She couldn't keep running. Making a decision, she picked up the phone, got an outside line, then called the police emergency number.

Giving her name and location, she told the dispatcher about the two men who had been following her. Then added a warning.

"I'm positive they're professionals."

Watching from a corner of the window, she saw the police car move slowly toward the parked car. Stopping a few feet away, the state troopers got out and stood staring from behind their opened doors.

"Get out of the car," one of them shouted.

There was a pause, and suddenly the engine of the car with the assailants came to life with a roar and started moving toward the law enforcement men.

Revealing the Mossberg 12 gauge shotguns with police grips they were carrying, the state troopers opened fire at the windshield of the charging vehicle.

While the driver hunched down behind the wheel, his partner shoved a 9 mm Uzi automatic out of his open window and washed the front of the troopers' car with hot lead.

Jumping out of the way, the officers continued to return fire at the oncoming vehicle.

With a violent crash, the dark sedan plowed into the front end of the state car, then came to a halt.

The face of the gunman in the front was covered with blood, and the driver had slumped over the wheel.

Moving with caution, the uniformed troopers closed in on the car. With a last effort, the gunman in the passenger seat shoved his weapon through the broken window in a last desperate attempt.

A barrage of fire from the shotguns stopped him and threw him back against the seat, a limp, broken body splattered with crimson.

Valerie drew back from the window.

Quickly she packed the small suitcase she had brought and started to leave the room. At the door already, she changed her mind. She went to the telephone sitting on the desk, intending to call Jim Holaday. Instead she dialed information.

She started to ask for the telephone number of the DEA, then decided to see if she could use an old contact instead.

"The telephone number of the Central Intelligence Agency," she said, when the operator came on the line.

When she had been put through, the voice that answered denied any knowledge of a Hiram Wilson.

"If you locate him, tell him that Valerie Wilding, whom he knew in Vietnam, has important information he might find useful."

"Could you leave your telephone number?"

"I'll call him back in a few days," she said, hanging up before she could be asked any more questions.

HOGAN FELT the cool cloth on his forehead. When he started to feel pain in his left arm and side, he remembered the battle and wondered how Brom was.

He opened his eyes and saw the delicate face framed by hair the color of unripe strawberries. It was Astrah.

She looked worried, despite her smile.

"Your eyes have been closed for a day," she said. "How do you feel?"

Black Jack groaned. "As though Brom sat on me."

He heard a laugh from his right and turned his head. The red-bearded warrior was nearby, lying on pillows.

"If I sat on you, you would have more than some slashes on your body," the Kalabrian said.

Black Jack Hogan looked around. He was in a large room constructed of giant blocks of stone. A huge fireplace dominated the far wall. On the remaining walls hung long banners of silk and wool.

He knew where he was. In Brom's private chambers at the palace in Tella, the capital of Kalabria.

A tall, flaxen-haired woman in a thick tunic and wide pants was kneeling next to Brom. Hogan recognized her as Mora, Brom's woman.

She glanced at him coldly. "Every time you come, Hogan, there are battles, injuries and death."

There was a hardness about Mora that came from her devotion to Brom as well as from her training as the leader of the dance warriors, the elite troop of women trained as performers and soldiers.

Astrah sounded annoyed as she spoke up. "That is not fair, Mora. It is Brom who is responsible for Hogan coming here to save him."

Mora glared at her, while Brom roared with laughter at her expression.

"You have been training the temple maiden well, Mora. Astrah stands up to you as no man who would dare."

Until Mora took her on as an apprentice, Astrah had been a temple maiden, helping the priests of Kalabria with their religious duties. After Hogan had entered her life, she asked Brom's mate-to-be to train her to become a dance warrior like herself.

The hint of a smile showed on Mora's face as she looked at Astrah. "What you say is true. These two together are impossible. All they seem to do is get into fights."

"And who knows what they do when they are together or not with us," Astrah agreed.

Brom lifted his head and studied the visitor from another world. "How do you spend your time away from Kalabria, Hogan?"

"Trying to stay alive."

There was a hint of jealousy in Astrah's voice as she asked, "Protecting yourself from the anger of other women?"

Hogan explained about the attacks, then added, "I intend to find out who is behind it. For the sake of Grisolm and his family."

Astrah nodded with understanding as she checked the bandages. "At least the bleeding has stopped. But you will have to lie still for a few days or you will tear open the threads Mora used to sew you together when you were brought here."

A servant brought in two large bowls and set them down beside the stacks of pillows on which the two wounded men were lying.

Hogan glanced at the bowl near him and wondered what was in it. In a minute Astrah sat down next to him and began to feed him with a spoon. Hogan took a mouthful of the hot concoction and spat it out.

"That's terrible. What is it?"

From the cushions nearby, Brom voiced similar indignation. "This mush is food for an infant, not for a man."

Mora eyed him coldly. "When you are physically well enough to behave like a man, you will be ready to eat a man's food."

Astrah listened to the words and turned to Hogan.

"This applies to you, too."

There was a determination in her voice that surprised Black Jack. The shyness she had displayed when he first saw her was rapidly disappearing.

"No," he said quietly, and let her feed him the balance of the gruel.

Afterwards, the American pulled himself up in a sitting position and saw his long knife and .44 magnum revolver sitting on a low table near him. Reaching for both, he tried to get to his feet.

"Rest a few days," Astrah pleaded with him. "I have seen so little of you."

Feeling very weak, Hogan allowed her to lower him to the pillows. She lay down beside him and gently massaged his neck.

Brom watched them, then turned to Mora with a grin. "Obviously, it is time for me to move from this room."

Mora glanced at her protégée and the alien warrior.

"Why? You may get some new ideas if we stayed, my lord," she said lightly, though her face remained expressionless.

Brom gave her a glittering look, then reached for the long rope that signaled the servants to come and help him.

Hogan and Astrah heard none of this. "Rest, Hogan," she said in a whisper. "Let me make you feel better."

Minutes after the servants carried Brom out of the room on a pallet, with Mora following beside him, Astrah proceeded to make good her promise. She was so sweet, so warm and tender, that Hogan felt he had landed in heaven.

HIRAM WILSON listened silently to the call from Calvin Dirken, one of the operations directors at the CIA.

"Valerie Wilding?" The name sounded familiar. "What did she want?"

Dirken explained she wouldn't give his man any details. Only that she had information she was sure Wilson wanted.

Wilson suddenly remembered where he had heard the name before. In Saigon. Major Wilding, aide to

General Holaday. He hadn't thought about her for more than ten years.

"Did you check her out?"

"Of course," Dirken replied. "She's been having an affair with Holaday ever since they retired from the air force. At least she was having an affair with him until she moved back to Washington and started going out with other men."

"Sounds like her information is about Holaday. What's he been up to?"

"He's been living on a ranch in west Texas."

Wilson was surprised. Generals usually didn't have the kind of money it took to buy a ranch in Texas unless they came from a family with money. And Holaday didn't.

"Raising cattle?"

"No, he leases the land out."

"I can't imagine he can keep operating the ranch on that and what he gets from his retirement fund."

"He was running a small organization called the Military Preparedness Association out of his home. From what we can learn, it was well endowed. Maybe he draws a salary."

"Any idea who's backing him?"

"Only rumors. One of them is that a General Soong has made donations through some front corporations."

The White House aide whistled. "Soong from Laos?"

The response was affirmative.

"One of the warlords of Indochina. Is he still growing opium?"

"More than ever."

"And he's backing Holaday's organization? Strange company for James Mattoon Holaday to keep."

"Our records show they worked together during the war."

Wilson remembered. He had made the deal with the Laotian. Soong would provide landing fields for CIA-recruited teams of Hmong hill tribesmen in exchange for allowing him to use overseas military transport planes. Holaday had objected but, under pressure from the Pentagon, finally agreed to go along with the arrangement.

Wilson wondered why Soong would put money into Holaday's organization.

"Tell me about the Military Preparedness Association."

"They've got a quarrel with the administration because they ended the Cold War with the Russkies and their buddies. Their literature claims the government is selling us down the river with their pacifist attitudes."

Even in Vietnam, Wilson remembered the general ranting about the limitations the government had set on his response to North Vietnam attacks. As much as he had sympathized with Holaday's frustrations, he had to keep reminding him that the President, not the generals, set the policy for the country.

But he still had no clue why the former Major Valerie Wilding was desperately trying to reach him.

"Give her my number if she calls again," he said.

"Will do, Hiram," Dirket promised, then remembered something. "One last bit of information. The name Arnold Becker mean anything to you?"

"Becker?" Wilson racked his memory. "The only Becker I know was a Special Forces sergeant who ran mercenaries in Laos and Cambodia. There was some rumor that he had a connection to Soong's operation."

"That's the one."

"What about him?"

"He's been working for General Holaday since Vietnam."

Suddenly it seemed to Wilson that it would be easier to look at the bottom of a muddy pool than trying to find a connection to the separate bits of information.

"Thanks for the information," Wilson said flatly, running his hand through his white hair. But after he hung up, he went to work, looking through file after file and making hasty telephone calls. Then he stared through his window, wondering just what he'd stumbled across.

11

Black Jack saw the disappointed expression on Astrah's face as the glowing fog surrounded him. As she had promised, she had taken charge of their love-making with a new confidence and strength he had not sensed in her before.

Truly she was a woman worthy of a warrior. She had nursed him back to health and given him a strong part of herself. He had never met anyone like her—in this world or in his own.

Then, before he could voice his feelings to her, she and Kalabria vanished.

Hogan was surprised to find himself back in his Jeep. The air had a faint glimmer to it, but in a few seconds it dissipated. His weapons were piled on the seat beside him.

He looked around and suddenly stiffened. He spotted four men, apparently searching the Apache burial grounds near where their vehicle was parked. A fifth man sat behind the wheel of the idling Lincoln that had pulled up fairly close to his rented car—windows closed, the radio blasting.

The men stopped in their tracks and stared at him.

Their expressions were cold and hooded, stamped with dark intent. Hogan had seen the type many times in his life. Hired killers.

He started the Jeep, and the man in the car reached down, then his window started rolling down. Even as

Hogan shoved the shift into reverse, the snout of a 9 mm TEC-9 emerged from the Lincoln's interior.

He could see the men jump into the large car, which was already rolling forward. Hogan reached for the .44 Magnum Smith & Wesson revolver he wore at his side, then remembered he had just recently emptied the cartridges.

His sole weapons now were an almost-empty revolver, an Apache bow and arrows and the Kalabrian long knife. Not much defense against five well-armed killers, he warned himself.

Hogan shifted into first and shoved his foot down on the gas pedal. The Jeep exploded from the side of the road with a jackrabbit start as Black Jack expertly moved the steering wheel to prevent the vehicle from lurching into a spin.

The driver of the luxury sedan fed his car more gas, trying desperately to keep up with his quarry.

Hunched over the wheel, Hogan was peering around desperately, searching for the small cutoff he remembered from his teenage years. He had driven many girls down the narrow road for an evening of necking while he had been in high school.

Racing his Jeep around a bend in the road, Hogan spotted the almost-hidden dirt road. Low-hanging branches and overgrown shrubbery covered the entrance.

Twisting the steering wheel sharply, he charged into the side road and sped down the narrow path, tearing through the stands of cactus and ponderosa pine until he reached the dead end.

Grabbing the bow and quiver, he opened the door and jumped from the vehicle. Swiftly he faded into the shrubbery as he heard the sound of the large sedan coming closer.

The car stopped and all four doors flew open. The occupants scrambled out from the vehicle, hefting their automatic weapons.

The driver studied the hood of his car.

"Lookit—scratches on the hood. I'm gonna kill that son of a bitch for what he done to my car," he grumbled.

"Shut up, Marco," ordered another, a hefty man with scars on his face. "You'll make enough to buy two cars like that one on this job."

The driver looked around. "If we find him. This guy's supposed to be part Indian. Who knows where he's hiding."

The man with the scarred face laughed, then sprayed the woods in front of him with lead from his 9 mm Uzi automatic rifle.

"Ain't met an Indian—or anyone else—who could hide out very long from one of these babies," he sneered, affectionately patting the barrel of his weapon.

The other three moved to his side and aimed their automatic weapons at the thick shrubbery around them. In unison, they held their fingers on the triggers of their guns and laughed as metal pellets chewed up trees and bushes.

But Hogan had already moved to higher ground, searching for another exit. Behind him the land became a steep incline that was almost impossible to traverse without hiking boots. On the other three sides, the five men were slowly shuffling forward, emptying round after round, then snapping fresh clips into their weapons.

Five to one. He had only a slim chance, but a slim chance was better than none.

Silently Hogan slipped through the woods until he was behind the men.

Slipping the end of an arrow into the bowstring, he pulled the bow back into a deep curve and waited.

Some distance ahead of him, a peeved voice called out, "Any sight of him, Emilio?"

"Nope, but he's got to be around here. He couldn't vanish into thin air," the man yelled back.

"I got a couple of smoke grenades in the car," the driver shouted. "Let's see if we can smoke him out."

The driver emerged into view from the thick shrubbery. In his right arm he cradled a 9 mm TEC-9 automatic.

Hogan waited until the man looked up and saw him, then released the arrow.

Before the hit man could shout a warning, the feathered shaft tore into his throat and rammed its pointed tip out the back of his neck. The gunman tried to tear the arrow from his throat with clawed fingers, then suddenly collapsed.

Hogan silently trotted to his side and scooped up the automatic weapon. Quickly checking the 30-round clip, he found it nearly full. Now the hunted could again become the hunter.

A voice called out from behind the trees. "Hey, Marco. Where are those smoke bombs?"

For a moment there was silence. Then somebody else loudly commented, "Either Marco's taking a leak or something's happened to him."

Black Jack heard the loud cracking of fallen branches as heavy feet trampled on them. They were moving in his direction. There was a curse as one of them stumbled, then the four men emerged from the woods and saw him.

"The son of a bitch is armed!" came a shouted warning as the quartet turned their weapons on him.

Hogan threw himself into a forward roll and came up behind the large Lincoln. Using the heavy vehicle as a shield, he waited for them to make a move.

"Spread out!" shouted a gunman, and they fanned out cautiously.

There was no solid cover nearby for Hogan. As he saw them move into position, he popped up from his crouching position and washed the ground around with a hail of lead.

A gunman halted in his tracks and stared in surprise at the hole in his chest. Holding his gun on the wound, he charged toward Hogan like an enraged bull. But another short spray of lead took him down for good.

The other three hit men kept up a steady stream of fire as they moved closer, dodging from boulder to boulder.

Hogan started to resume firing, but the weapon jerked in his hands as a dented casing jammed in the chamber. He tried to unjam the chamber, but was forced to the ground as a sheet of lead filled the air above him.

A new concern ran through his mind. How did the gunman know he would be at the burial grounds? Only his grandfather knew, and Wise Crow would die before he told a white man anything. Especially white men like these.

He stared at them—and saw the large crystal strung on a leather thong one of them wore around his neck. Wise Crow's treasured energy source. There was only one way he would have let it be taken from his person.

A bloodcurdling cry erupted from the woods, adding a new note to the battle sounds. It was followed by a staccato chatter, and one of the attackers leaped into the air as hot lead chewed him up.

Hogan risked a quick look and saw a familiar figure, all massive, towering muscle with hair and beard like a red beacon, standing with his legs spread in the middle of what seemed to be fading lightning. In his hands, looking somewhat out of place, was an AK-47.

"I thought you were out of ammunition," Hogan called out.

"I found more in my bag after you left." But Brom, oblivious to everything, spared no ammunition as he sprayed copious lead at the remaining hit men.

"You're wasting shots," Hogan shouted as he struggled with the chamber mechanism to free the bent cartridge.

"My fire-stick shall spit for as long as I need it," Brom replied, proudly.

The gunman who wore Wise Crow's crystal swung around to face the new enemy.

"Come. Eat your death," Brom taunted as he started to vent the anger of the automatic on the enemy. He stood staring in surprise when the weapon remained silent, and there was only the sound of metal clicking on an empty chamber.

"The fire-stick has run out of its metal poison," Brom complained loudly even as the gunman raised his Uzi automatic to fire.

There was no time to warn the bewildered-looking warrior who kept staring at the empty assault rifle.

Grabbing the long bow, Black Jack quickly notched an arrow into the gut string and pulled it back.

"For you, Wise Crow," he said softly as he released the arrow.

With a soft hum, the metal-tipped shaft flew across the field and tore into the chest of the man with the Uzi.

Seeing his buddy fall, the last of the hit squad turned his TEC-9 on Hogan.

"Die, bastard," he blathered in fear, then stared blankly as the long blade of a sword severed his head from his body in a shower of blood.

Brom rested the tip of his glistening sword on the ground, while Hogan moved swiftly to retrieve Wise Crow's crystal from around the neck of the dead assassin.

With the crystal in his hand, he looked at the fierce warrior who was kneeling and wiping the blood from his blade.

"Brom," Hogan said with a grin. "I was wondering if you'd show up."

"You picked an impossible moment to need my assistance," the red-bearded warrior said with a grimace. "Mora and I had settled down on the pillows when the call came."

Hogan smiled at Brom's complaint. "You could have chosen to stay."

"And miss this battle?" Brom made a face.

Hogan's smile faded as he studied the bloodstained crystal he held in his hand.

Brom glanced at it curiously. "What is it?"

"A crystal."

"Is it magic?"

"My grandfather thought so."

The red-bearded Kalabrian looked at the corpses on the ground. "And these carrions killed him?"

Black Jack nodded. "There was no other way he would have been parted from it."

Enraged, the fierce warrior swung his huge sword to decapitate a still body, but Hogan grabbed his wrist and stopped him.

"It won't bring Wise Crow back," he said sadly. Slowly he walked through the woods toward the burial grounds.

Brom followed behind, then stopped at the edge of the sacred land, as if he sensed when he had come to the point where only his spiritual twin could continue.

As the Kalabrian watched, Hogan went over to a small mound of rocks, then knelt. Using his long knife, he scooped out a trench in the hard ground. With reverence, he placed the crystal in the shallow grave, then covered it with fresh dirt.

For a brief moment Hogan bowed his head. Brom could have sworn he had detected a drop course down that hard face, but it vanished when Hogan got to his feet and rejoined him.

"Is this where your family is buried?"

Hogan waved a vague hand in the air. "All but me," he said with the hint of pain in his voice.

The Kalabrian leader understood. He also found it difficult to visit the gravesites of his parents, who had been murdered only a few years earlier.

"It's time to leave," Black Jack said quietly. "Both of us have things to do."

Hogan started to turn away, but stopped when he saw Brom move past him and kneel at the spot where the American had buried Wise Crow's necklace.

As Black Jack looked on in surprise, Brom dug with his hands and retrieved the crystal, then got up and walked back.

Handing Hogan the necklace, he commented, "Among my people, we remember those we love by wearing something that belonged to them." He fingered the large pendant around his neck. "This was my father's. And his father's before him." He looked at the crystal in Hogan's hand. "Wear the stone and remember the man who wore it before you."

As they made their way to the Jeep, Brom waited for Hogan to comment, but he remained silent.

"Perhaps you should return with me. Astrah can help ease the pain of your grandfather's passing. Remember, you two had come close in body and spirit."

The American shook his head, smiling gratefully at the invitation. "Tell her I will come back to her soon. After I find out who sent these men after me." He looked up at the sky before adding, "And I will revenge Wise Crow's death."

12

The summons from the Oval Office had made it clear to Hiram Wilson that he was wanted immediately. There was no time to ponder the information the CIA official had passed on to him and try to make sense of it.

When he arrived, the President's personal secretary ushered him inside.

The man behind the desk pointed to a chair, then waited for the secretary to leave and close the door before he spoke.

"Look at these," he said, standing and handing his intelligence aide a handful of photographs.

Normally Hiram Wilson wore the mask of an impeccably dressed, cherubic-looking man in his sixties. But not now. He looked stunned as he studied the dozen photographs.

Even to someone who had spent his life in intelligence work, the photographs were shocking. Corpses of men, women and children were sprawled across lawns, in backyards and playgrounds, in a shopping mall, inside the processing buildings and in the parking lot of the nuclear processing plant.

"Two thousand people died in Harwood, Texas, yesterday," the President said in a voice filled with pain and sadness. "Two thousand men, women and children were murdered."

Wilson took a minute before he asked a question. "How?"

"Technically uranium hexafluoride gas escaped and mingled with moist air to form a highly toxic gas." He looked down at his huge desk and picked up a single sheet of paper. "It could have been an accident...." He passed the sheet of paper across the desk to Wilson. "Except for three factors." Then he removed several photographs from a file folder stamped Eyes Only and handed them to his intelligence aide.

With narrowed eyes Wilson studied the photographs. Three were close-ups of three dead men in contamination suits with automatic rifles lying near them.

"The first is that, according to our inspection team, bullets from the weapons next to those men ruptured storage tanks at the nuclear plant in Harwood. What is strange is that the contamination suits worn by them had been sabotaged so that the gas could penetrate inside."

Wilson wondered why the President had shown him the photographs. "Who were the men, Mr. President? Members of the plant security force?"

"Not according to the FBI. The three men are long-time mercenaries." His eyes were clouded with confusion as he looked up and stared at the thick gold chain that hung from the pockets of Wilson's vest.

The stocky aide rolled his Cuban cigar between his fingers and said nothing. He could tell the President had more to say on the subject.

"If that wasn't enough to keep me worried for a long time, this is." He handed the senior intelligence aide a typewritten page.

Wilson scanned the page and quickly saw that it was a photostat of the threatening demand the United Nations official had received.

The white-haired man's face became cold with anger. "Who received this?"

"It was delivered to the aide to the secretary general." He glanced down at the memo that had accompanied the message. "A Jaako Rinmann. Former Swedish chargé d'affaires in Washington until he was asked to join the UN administration staff."

The man behind the large desk in the Oval Office kept rubbing the edge of his fist on his chin as he continued. "We can't keep this from our allies. They're all affected, Hiram."

Hiram Wilson shook his head. "Insanity. The world can't abandon nuclear mines and plants just because some crackpot hands out exaggerated threats." He raised his voice. "Millions of people depend on them for essential power, for vital cancer treatments. And the military would never stand for it."

"What exaggerated threats? Two thousand civilians are dead."

Wilson bowed his head in acknowledgment. "I know, Mr. President. What do you want done?"

"I'm fresh out of ideas. I can't send the Army to attack an invisible enemy. That's why I asked you to join me. Have you got any suggestions?"

For a moment Wilson wondered if the information Major Wilding was so anxious to give him had anything to do with Harwood. Then he decided he was jumping to conclusions. He stood up and wandered to the large window at the opposite side of the room.

Through it he could see the thin granite needle of the Washington Monument.

Across the broad green lawns, he thought he could make out the long black monument dedicated to the memory of the young men and women who had died in Vietnam.

For what? he wondered. What would they have said to such demands?

He thought for a while, then made a decision.

He walked back toward the desk.

"Let Black Jack find out who's behind the massacre and handle them."

Black Jack Hogan was officially a nonperson. As far as the administration was concerned, no one by that name worked for them in any capacity.

But as the man in the Oval Office knew, when all other efforts had failed in past catastrophes, Hogan had eliminated the threat and the cause of it.

"Will he accept the mission? As I remember, your agreement with him is that he can refuse an assignment."

Wilson gently rolled the Cuban cigar in his hand between his fingers and smiled with assurance. He remembered Hogan's insistence on going to Harwood when he heard the news.

"He'll accept it."

"It can't be official," the solemn-faced Chief Executive warned.

Wilson nodded.

"And he knows this?"

"He prefers it that way."

Looking relieved, the President stood up and held out a hand. Wilson shook it.

"You're confident he can solve the problem?"

"I have every confidence he will," Wilson said with assurance.

To himself he added silently, because God help all of us if he doesn't.

13

Phineas Smith had been waiting in his small Toyota across from Bangkok's Don Muang Airport, watching all morning for John Hogan to come out of the terminal building. He knew exactly what the man looked like.

Hogan was a living legend among the career professionals at the American Embassy in Bangkok. Many of the younger men and women had served in Vietnam and knew of his reputation. He got the job done, and—more important—survived.

Until last night he had been a hero to Smith, too. But that had been before he'd taken on this job. After all, a man had to make a living. First things first.

Smith checked his watch again.

9:00 a.m.

The Northwest flight from the United States was supposed to have landed ten minutes ago, but the heavy summer rains had delayed arriving flights for the past twenty-four hours.

FINDING OUT when Hogan was supposed to arrive had been easy. He had asked Howard Lancaster, the resident intelligence agent.

"I haven't heard you complain about Black Jack Hogan for weeks. Anything wrong?"

The CIA officer was famous around the American Embassy for his continuous complaints that he had been sent to his personal purgatory having to baby-sit Hiram Wilson's field agent. Hogan's reckless disregard for personal safety had made Lancaster's already thinning head of hair that much thinner. The only thing that helped him maintain his sanity was the knowledge that he would be able to file his retirement papers within six months.

"He was on medical leave in the United States. But he's due in later this morning," Lancaster moaned. "And I'm supposed to make sure he calls Washington the minute he arrives. They've called twice last night and three times this morning." He looked at his visitor with a woebegone expression. "My ulcer can't take much more of Hogan."

Smith saw an opportunity to pick up some extra cash for confidential information. "Sounds like something is up."

"Nobody tells me anything, but you're right. Something big must be cooking. The calls came directly from the White House."

The agricultural attaché wondered if that slim bit of news would be worth something, then decided he would concentrate on his original assignment.

"Hey, I've got to get the literature from the Department of Agriculture that's coming in on the morning flight from the United States. Maybe I can pick him up for you," he said with enthusiasm. "I'd like to meet this character who's driving you nuts."

"You're welcome to him." Lancaster's eyes brightened with hope. "I mean, all you have to do is get him back here the minute his plane lands."

"No sweat."

Smith rose and eagerly headed for the door.

"One thing," the intelligence officer called out.

Phineas Smith turned back, his hand already on the doorknob. What hitch was coming? he wondered.

"Don't let him stop and make a call, whatever you do. Or else Hogan will decide to take a detour to stop and visit with one of his female friends, and I'll be stuck trying to explain to Washington why he isn't here."

The agricultural attaché had heard about Black Jack Hogan's female companions. Most of them were attractive, lonely women who were ready to put up with his infrequent appearances.

Smith envied the special agent. No one had ever tried to solicit him for a night of fun and games. Not even his wife, Edith.

Then he had a consoling thought. No woman would solicit Hogan again after tomorrow.

THE CUSTOMIZED RIFLE was propped up against the seat next to him. It was less than eighty yards from where he sat to the entrance doors to the terminal. He had paced the distance earlier.

He'd received five thousand dollars in advance from the Cambodian who had contacted him minutes before he was scheduled to leave his office last night. He had barely enough time to line up a team of professionals to back him up.

As it was, he'd arrived a half hour late for dinner, which started one of the endless fights Edith and he had had since he'd requested a transfer here fifteen years ago.

He couldn't explain to her about how he was able to bring home the extra money she always seemed to need. To explain would mean he had to tell her that he had spent years training himself to be the caliber marksman who could command large fees for assassination assignments.

Edith didn't really care how he earned the money. She had been harping for months about buying a new car. The one he was driving kept breaking down. But no private assignments had been offered to him until now.

The salary he received as an agricultural attaché was barely adequate. Even with the housing allowance.

He shut his thoughts off when he saw the terminal doors open. Quickly he grabbed his rifle and propped it on the opened window.

Pushing his eyes against the scope, he stared at the emerging figure. It was the Cambodian who had hired him. That was the signal that the target was on his way out of the terminal.

Smith watched the client dart aside, out of the line of fire.

Smith searched around the outside of the terminal for the three men he had hired.

He saw one of them, in a chauffeur's uniform, leaning against an official Embassy car. During working hours, Tim McKanter was an ex-marine guard at the American Embassy who now worked for a local exporter of Thai silk.

Souvanna Phoursan, the short, wiry Thai from the north of the country who supervised the housekeeping staff, was standing at the curb, arguing with another Thai who Phineas Smith knew to be his brother-in-law.

Each of them was armed and ready to whip out his concealed weapon.

Then the terminal door opened again.

Smith studied the man who came out. It was Hogan.

There was an unmistakable look about the counterinsurgency specialist. Tall but not gangly, the man was a mass of well-developed muscles under his deeply tanned skin. He carried no extra bulk, but Smith knew the man possessed enormous power and battle expertise.

He studied the face of the new arrival. The strongly marked Indian features were a startling contrast to the dark blond hair that hung down almost to his shoulders. But even more distinctive were his eyes. They were almost colorless.

He had stared at them every time Hogan had come into the Embassy to meet with Lancaster.

Hogan's appearance suited the near-legend surrounding him. But that living legend was about to die, Smith thought as he rested his finger on the hair trigger and moved the rifle slightly to the left. As he pulled his finger gently back, he felt the presence of someone behind him.

Turning his head, he saw a huge head with glowing red hair look around in bewilderment at the traffic around the terminal, then turn and give him a piercing stare. Before Smith could get a word out of his mouth, a powerful arm raised a long, wide sword and severed his head from his body.

BLACK JACK glanced up and was surprised to see the red-bearded Kalabrian standing by the small Japanese car. He started to cross the roadway to join him when Brom raised the customized rifle he had snatched from inside the vehicle and held it over his head.

From a corner of his eye, Hogan saw the chauffeur standing at the Embassy car displaying the American flag reach under his jacket. Hogan immediately dodged behind the long black vehicle before the chauffeur's .45 ACP Colt Government cleared leather.

Cautiously the assassin held the large pistol in front of him as he moved slowly toward the rear end of the government car.

Hogan waited until he saw the outstretched arm come into his view, then balanced his body and threw a side kick at the wrist holding the gun.

The Colt flew through the air in an arc. Furious, the man turned to face Hogan and with an angry snarl launched himself at his target.

Hogan sidestepped, then aimed a cowboy-booted toe just below the attacker's kneecap.

Grunting with shock and pain, the assassin fell to his knees, and Black Jack threw a carefully aimed kick behind his right ear. One down, Hogan thought, but how many more to go?

Twisting toward Hogan, another assailant revealed the short Israeli-made Uzi he had been carrying under his loose-fitting jacket and released a burst of fire.

Diving to the ground, Hogan rolled out of the path of the death-seekers spitting from the muzzle of the weapon, then grabbed the .45 ACP Colt and quickly returned fire.

Four bullets churned from the muzzle of the heavy handgun. Three of them tore into the gunman's body, carving a deadly path to his vital organs.

Blood spouted from the wounds, and Hogan rolled behind the mortally wounded man to shield himself from the stream of hot metal spewing his way from an AK-47 held by the remaining attacker.

A long knife appeared from nowhere and spun through the air. Expertly thrown, the surgically sharp blade thunked into the chest of the man with the AK-47. He dropped his automatic weapon so he could tear the offending metal from his lungs.

Pink froth pumped from the gaping wound as he dropped the knife and unsuccessfully tried to stem the bleeding with his bare hands. But his efforts were short-lived, and he crumpled into a motionless heap.

Brom dragged himself to where his bloodied knife had fallen and scooped it up, then glanced at Hogan.

"How could you get in so much trouble so quickly? Until minutes ago you were in the belly of the metal bird."

"Luck, I guess."

From far off, they heard the sounds of police sirens. When Hogan looked around, he realized that a small crowd of shocked bystanders had gathered and were staring at them.

A shabbily dressed Cambodian sized up the scene in disgust. In a minute he became aware that the two warriors were looking at him and quickly shuffled back inside the terminal.

Lon Nol knew he would have to call General Soong and give him the news. He shuddered at what the Laotian's reaction would be.

"I think you better leave before the cops get here," Hogan said in a low voice.

Brom stared at him, an expression of puzzlement on his face.

Black Jack realized the expression was foreign to the Kalabrian. "Before the soldiers get here and start asking questions," he added.

Brom scooped up some clips from the dead man's waistband and stuffed them into his clothes. "Perhaps you should return with me."

"There are things I need to find out here."

"Then until we meet, my friend," Brom said, and started to move away. The crowd turned away after parting to make room for him, and the next second he was gone.

Hogan shrugged for the benefit of the shocked bystanders and stalked into the terminal, heading for the pay phones to place his call to the American Embassy.

14

Hiram Wilson was livid. Jack Hogan had managed to slip out of Bangkok without calling him.

For a moment he wondered if Lancaster had really given the agent the message to call him. His Bangkok man swore he had. But he also mentioned that Hogan had seemed to have sustained some injuries.

Hogan should have been more careful, Wilson grumbled to himself as he lifted the phone and snapped at Mrs. Bolivar, the motherly woman who had been his secretary since he joined the permanent White House staff, to place another call to the radio telephone he had installed in the temple of Angkor Wat.

Although he knew Black Jack was the would-be victim and not the attacker, the White House aide wanted to chew out the large man with long dark blond hair about the trail of bodies he had left behind him. Two sets in Arizona and the quartet in Bangkok. There was just so much he could cover up before he ran out of favors owed him.

Especially the killing of an attaché at the American Embassy. Except for the customized hunting rifle, there was no evidence that he had anything to do with the others involved in the attempt to kill Hogan.

For a moment Wilson wondered if the army shrinks who had examined Black Jack Hogan when he had been discharged from active duty for medical reasons were right after all. They had said the counterinsurgency specialist was too unstable to be trusted with military secrets that could embarrass the government.

No one had actually seen his man behead the agricultural attaché. The only possible link was that similar accidents had occurred when Hogan was present.

Wilson was in an awkward spot. The Secretary of State had gone to the President to demand that Hogan be brought to Washington and questioned. In turn, the Chief Executive had called Wilson in and announced that he agreed with his Secretary of State.

There was no point arguing with the tall, lean man who occupied the private quarters of the White House. His reputation for stubbornness had helped him get elected, and reelected.

Wilson knew that an investigation could take months. And the country might not have that much time to wait and still remain "the land of the free," as the national anthem had promised.

No, he needed to meet with Black Jack as soon as possible. They would have to meet someplace outside the country.

The answer was obvious.

He opened the door and saw Mrs. Bolivar patiently holding the phone to her ear for the call to Cambodia to be completed.

She saw Wilson looking at her and turned to face him.

"After you get Hogan, call the people at Andrews Air Force Base and arrange a flight for me to Bangkok."

MOK SENG PLACED the telephone against his ear again and repeated the same words for the third time.

"Hogan is not here."

The man from Washington continued to insist he wanted to talk to Hogan immediately.

Dealing with the uncultured Caucasians was a challenge to his serenity. Even Hogan, who had begun to show signs of shedding his Western attitudes, still frequently reverted to the savage combatant he had been when he first came to the temple as a wounded soldier. But at least the large American seemed to be learning some patience.

At their last session before Hogan left for the United States to have his body explored by the barbaric doctors of his government, the abbot had felt his student was ready to aspire to the next level of his understanding of the way of the Buddha.

After the mandatory practice of the ancient and civilized art of Cambodian unarmed combat and the proper use of the bow and sword, he had sat with Hogan before the gilded statue of Buddha and shared with him his wisdom.

"The way of the journey is difficult, but the elephant is patient."

He had been disappointed to see a puzzled expression on the American's face. To imagine someone having a life experience of almost forty years and still be unable to comprehend so simple a thought had astounded Mok Seng.

"What does it mean?"

"It means you must be patient."

"Oh," Hogan had replied flatly. "I guess it was different when that was written. Everything moved slower then. If I get too patient, I may wake up dead again. But thanks for the quote from Buddha.''

Mok Seng sighed. The lesson had gone unlearned. He wondered if he had read the saying in one of the holy works or heard it in an American movie.

It didn't matter, he'd decided. If Buddha hadn't said it, he should have.

Mok Seng had given way to his train of thought and was surprised when a young monk pushed open his door and rushed inside.

"A helicopter is landing in the fields east of the temple," he announced breathlessly.

The elderly abbot stared with disapproval. "For this minor news, you interrupt me?"

Blurting out apologies, the Buddhist monk bowed his way out of the abbot's study.

Through the window Mok Seng surveyed the ruins of the ancient city of Angkor Wat and the dense jungle that surrounded the monastery. Hogan had returned. There would be no other reason for a helicopter to land near the temple.

He would give Hogan the message from Washington. But not right away. First he wanted to make sure the American was well.

He had sensed that somehow he had been physically damaged and needed to return to the meditation that brought serenity before he imparted the news that would lead back to battle.

BLACK JACK LAY on the narrow cot in the cell that had become his home at the temple. He winced with pain as the elderly monk prodded his body with his fingers.

"That hurts," he complained.

"You have become a child since you left this sacred place," the abbot chastised.

"You try having people shoot and slash swords and knives at you just because you're Mok Seng and see how you feel after they're done."

"Tell me what happened," the abbot said.

Hogan reviewed the journey after he left Washington. The death of Charley Grisolm and his family. The attempted assassinations in Arizona and in Bangkok.

Ever since Hogan had become a special intelligence operative for the United States government, he had been a target for assassins, but what had surprised him, he told Mok Seng, was the attack on sacred tribal burial grounds. "My grandfather told me that not even the drug dealers who sometimes hang out in the woods would dare go there."

"Americans are savages," the bald-headed monk commented bluntly. "Who knows what a savage will do. No Cambodian will think of violating sacred places, no matter what the reason."

"Not even the remnants of the Khmer Rouge murder squads who still roam the countryside?"

"They were raised Buddhist," the small monk replied crisply. "Even they respect the sanctity of a Buddhist temple."

Hogan reminded him of something that had happened several months earlier. "Wasn't it the Khmer Rouge who had sent a child into the temple to plant a poisonous snake and kill me?"

Mok Seng refused to reply to Black Jack's comment. Instead, he directed a question of his own to the

American. "Do you believe that all of what has happened to you was because you are Hogan?"

"You mean about the Khmer Rouge?"

Mok Seng looked annoyed. "You keep dwelling on these brigands like a dog gnawing at a bone." His tone became haughty. "I was referring to your journey back to your uncivilized land."

"Got a better explanation?"

Mok Seng remembered something he had read. "Since you have become an infant again, perhaps you will understand this," he said in a patient tone. "Life is like a school, and it is filled with many children like yourself. But each of them is blindfolded and waves a sharp knife aimlessly in the air. As you wander through this school, there will be times when you will get cut. Did you get cut because you are you, or because you happen to be in the way?"

"Because I'm me," Hogan announced in reply. "And you can tell Buddha that for me."

"Do not blame Buddha for the question. An American doctor at Harvard University asked it."

"Well, you can tell the doctor to get into a fight with someone who wants to kill him and see if he still wonders if the other guy's shooting at him just because he happens to be in the way."

"But if you were a man of peace instead of a man of war, you would not be in the way," Mok Seng replied, and pressed down hard on a pressure point to ease muscular tension.

Hogan nearly jumped from the hard cot as his nerves reacted. He turned his head and shot Mok Seng a baleful look.

"Okay, so everyone's trying to kill me because I'm in their way."

"Good. Now that you understand, you should consider the American expression 'make love, not war.'"

Hogan shook his head in amusement. The monk was not only a master in Oriental armed and unarmed combat, and a philosopher, but he was also a collector of corny American expressions.

"I thought," he replied with a grin, "that Buddhist monks weren't allowed to make love."

"You still think like a barbarian." The aged abbot sniffed in disgust as he turned and walked to the door. "I shall return with healing salves and massage."

He stopped at the thick wooden door and looked coldly at the American lying on the cot.

"How much massage I decide you require to bring your body back in balance will depend on how much you meditate on your errors before I return."

As Mok Seng vanished through the door, Black Jack understood the message behind the words.

How convincing he was in asking forgiveness for implying that the elderly cleric wasn't celibate would determine how intensely the monk would manipulate his sore body with his amazingly strong fingers.

The flowery speech of apology he had begun to compose in his head was interrupted by a messenger notifying him that the man named Wilson was calling for him on the radio telephone for the fourth time that day.

15

It had been a hell of a day so far, James Holaday told himself as he opened a bottle and poured a shot of whiskey neat. He could only hope it would end better than it had started.

His public-relations firm had released his statement about the attack on Harwood, Texas. In it, he had blamed the administration's wishy-washy attitude toward criminals for what had happened.

But the press pickup had been less than satisfactory. Newspapers like the *New York Times* and *Washington Post* ignored his statement completely. But he considered those to be Communist-run. Even the newspaper in El Paso had only printed a small part of it on the page facing the obituaries.

That would all change after he went on television and proposed a solution to the crisis. His speech would come after several more attacks on nuclear plants—and the public would be more receptive to his message.

Soong had called from Vientiane to report that the contractor he had hired had missed Hogan in Bangkok. And to demand that Holaday have Becker find someone capable of killing the elusive American. Then he announced that he had decided to resume shipments despite Holaday's pleas to suspend them until after his television speech.

After all, it wouldn't do for the head of the emergency government to be dealing in drugs. In fact, he would probably have to put Soong out of business *permanently* so the Oriental couldn't decide to blackmail him.

He wondered what Soong would say if he knew what he was planning.

Probably burst a blood vessel and die, which would save him the trouble of having Becker do it.

Becker was another problem. The men he had recruited lately had consistently failed, with the exception of the team sent to Harwood.

Speak of the devil, Holaday thought when the door to his office opened and Becker walked in with the news that Valerie Wilding had vanished. There had been no trace of her since the hired guns got involved in a shoot-out at the Maryland motel with a pair of state troopers.

Holaday jumped from the chair behind the huge desk and exploded when Becker told him the news. "Hire better men to find her!" Then he thought of something. "Any sign she's contacted Wilson yet?"

"She tried. Our contact in the CIA said she placed a call to him, but wouldn't leave a number."

"Make sure the two of them are kept apart."

"She won't find him. I've had a man keeping an eye on the White House. Wilson headed out for the Andrews Air Force Base this morning and boarded a military jet. My man got chatting with one of the ground crew. The jet's heading for Bangkok. My guess is that Hogan will be heading there, too."

Holaday's eyes brightened at the news. He had something to trade with Soong in exchange for holding up on shipments. "You concentrate on finding Valerie Wilding. I'll handle Wilson and Hogan."

Becker grunted and walked out.

Holaday kept staring at the door. He would have to find a replacement for Becker. The man was getting sloppy.

He started running through a list of names in his head when the phone rang. Annoyed at the interruption, he picked it up. Angrily he snapped, "Yes?"

"This is Vigilante," the voice said.

Instantly the general became calm. "How can I help you?"

"I must see you."

"But I've scheduled to deliver my speech in two days—"

The voice on the other end interrupted him. "Contact the others and order them to meet you on the island. Then you can reschedule your speech."

Holaday began to protest. He wanted to explain that postponing his address would cost the millionaire a small fortune.

"Don't worry about the money. There's much more where that came from."

Holaday was stunned. There were times when he wondered if the man was more than human. How else could anybody know what he was about to say?

"I'll expect you tomorrow," the voice said, and hung up.

He'd have to leave Becker in charge, no matter how incompetent the man was. He had no other choice.

Almost like a robot, the retired general automatically lifted the phone and dialed the travel agency he used.

THE PAINTED LETTERS on the wooden door of the shop on the narrow side street were faded. Lon Nol Importing Company.

There were many similar-looking shop fronts on the winding, garbage-filled back streets of Phnom Penh. Small businessmen, who lived in rooms behind their stores, tried desperately to survive the shaky economy of the Cambodian capital.

Only a dim light that showed around the edges of the window blinds of the shop indicated there was any life inside.

At a ramshackle desk, a worried-looking man wiped perspiration from his brow as he spoke into the telephone.

"I hired the best, General Soong. The American Embassy man has worked for me before with great success."

The accented voice on the other end was more cold than angry. "I have read the newspaper accounts of the airport incident. Why is the American still alive?"

Lon Nol could feel the panic in his intestines. Suddenly he had the uncontrollable urge to rush to the bathroom. "I don't know, but I can hire more men," he said hastily.

"No. Hogan will be dealt with another way," the calm response came.

"But what about my fee? I have had great expenses."

"It is on its way."

Lon Nol heard the phone click on the other end. Exhausted, he leaned back in his chair.

He would send money to the families of the two Thais once he received the money. That way he would have made peace with the spirits that had inhabited their bodies.

GENERAL SOONG was in a rage. For weeks he had waited for the right moment to get Hogan. Now it had come and gone several times, and he was still alive.

"Like a cat with nine lives," he said in anger, then realized that Major Somchan had just entered the handsomely appointed office.

"Sorry to interrupt, General," he said. "But the manager at the plant in Phong Saly called and said the warehouse was full. The Hmong have broken in twice in the last two days. Where do you want him to store the rest of the production?"

The small city was located near the border with China. The Hmong tribesmen worked for Soong during the day, tending his poppy fields, then tried to break into his guarded warehouse and steal the processed opium from him at night.

"Tell him to rent any empty storeroom until I can make arrangements for shipping," he yelled.

"It will only encourage the Hmong to attempt to rob you again."

If Soong hadn't been frustrated, he would have been amused by the irony of the major's comment. It took a Hmong to understand how the Hmong tribesmen thought.

"There is nothing I can do about it. For now."

The major looked surprised. "I thought you had an arrangement with—"

Soong stopped him before he could finish the sentence. "I am making other arrangements." He let his eyes wander around his lavishly furnished office as his mind sorted through alternative options. The walls were covered with framed photographs of himself with famous foreigners.

His eyes stopped on an eight-by-ten photograph of himself with an elegantly attired American. Hiram Wilson, of the American CIA.

The two of them had worked closely during the recent war. Wilson was a practical man. He would always make a deal if the other person had something worthwhile to trade.

The general weighed the confidential information he carried around in his head. Which of the things he knew would be valuable enough to convince the American Intelligence officer to provide transportation and storage for his merchandise?

Suddenly it was obvious. He knew exactly what to trade. He could always find another American distributor. And, as he thought about it, he much preferred the money he made than the power Holaday had promised him.

He looked up and saw the young aide still staring at him.

"I ordered you to contact the manager of the plant," he growled.

Smartly the young officer snapped a salute and left.

Soong unlocked his center drawer and took out his confidential telephone directory. Turning the pages, he found Wilson's private number. There was, after all, something he could do on his own.

As soon as Wilson called him back his opium would be airborne and his Swiss bank account would grow even more substantial.

As he looked around the empty shop, Lon Nol wondered how soon he would be paid. Before he could think about it any further, he heard the front window crack.

Jumping to his feet, he rushed to the door. The orphaned children who lived on the streets of Phnom Penh had broken his window before. This time he would catch them.

As he got to the front door, he stopped and stared at the floor. There was a piece of soft gray clay stuck to a large sack of metal pieces.

Lon Nol recognized it. Plastique. He moved quickly to grab the bag and throw it through the broken window and into the street.

As his left hand grabbed the rough hemp sack, the soft plastic exploded and tore his body into unidentifiable chunks of tissue and bones.

Outside, a small boy watched from inside a doorway across the street. Through street-hardened eyes, he saw bits of glass, wood and brick spew out into the street. Then he recognized the bits of bloodied tissue and bone that were part of the fountain of death.

Swiftly the child ran down the street to where the uniformed Laotian officer was waiting in a rented car.

The officer had promised him the equivalent of twenty dollars American. A virtual fortune.

16

Hogan had declined Wilson's offer to send a helicopter to fetch him from the temple. Instead, he traveled to the Cambodian border sitting in the closed back of a surplus army truck, then paid a Thai motorcyclist to give him a ride to the Oriental Hotel.

As they came within a few streets of the luxury hotel, Hogan got a feeling of sadness as if someone he cared about were in great pain. For a moment he thought of the red-bearded warrior and hoped everything was all right with him.

As the motorcycle pulled up to the curb in front of the hotel, Wilson emerged through the front door.

Hogan grabbed the small bag he had brought and jumped off the bike.

Wilson looked at him with a smile. "Who do you think you are? One of the Hell's Angels?"

"More like one of hell's rejects," Hogan quipped. "What's up?"

Wilson signaled for a waiting Embassy car to pull up.

"I'll tell you on the way to the airport."

"Airport?"

"We're flying to Vientiane."

As Black Jack followed the man from Washington into the large car, the strange foreboding feeling returned. But there was no time for delay—destiny was calling.

THE MILITARY JET was already airborne. Sitting next to Wilson, Hogan was anything but bored by the reports and photographs Wilson had handed him. He kept thinking of Charley Grisolm and his family as he studied the photographs in Harwood. The awful scenes had driven thoughts of the most recent assassination attempt from his head.

He glanced behind him to see if Howard Lancaster was also looking at the photographs.

But the man was sound asleep.

Hogan turned back to the photographs. With cold fury in his voice, he asked, "What kind of butchers would have done something like this to innocent people?"

"We're going to meet somebody who may be able to give us the answer to that question," the white-haired man said.

"What's Lancaster here for?"

"To keep you out of trouble."

Hogan glanced back at the sleeping man. Lancaster didn't look as though he could even protect an old lady trying to cross a downtown street in Bangkok.

He turned back to the man from Washington.

"You don't have much taste in the talent you recruit," he cracked.

"I recruited you," Wilson replied with a straight face.

Hogan shut up and chalked one up for Wilson.

WRAPPING HIS HAND around his glass, Hogan shook his head as he took in the shabby interior of the White Poppy Bar. Howard Lancaster, next to him, kept a tight grip on the bottle of beer he had ordered and kept his eyes focused on it.

It had been more than fourteen years since Hogan was last in here, but nothing except the faces had changed. The huge room was crowded with the same kind of young prostitutes who draped themselves around the shoulders of mercenaries who had made the Laotian tavern their hangout since it opened.

There was one new addition. A jukebox blaring rock-and-roll music had replaced the usually drunk piano player who had been a fixture at the White Poppy fifteen years ago.

Wilson had told him to wait here with Lancaster while he had a meeting with someone.

Hogan thought of the elegant man who prided himself on his sartorial splendor. This place was not his usual hangout.

It had been built in the early seventies by a Frenchman who had escaped from the prison camp on Devil's Island and served cheap Algerian wines and simple Provençal cooking to French soldiers stationed in Vietnam. Later the White Poppy became the hangout for pilots who flew for the CIA-cover airline, Air America, in the days right before the Vietnamese war.

After the war it catered to mercenaries and prospective clients who were seeking hardmen to carry out executions, assassinations and a wide range of violent services.

Expatriates from almost every corner of the world had made the White Poppy their headquarters. French military officers who had managed to survive the overthrow of their puppet governments in Indochina,

Laotian government officials dropped in to negotiate a suitable bribe for their services—including looking the other way when a murder had to be committed.

Hogan glanced at Lancaster. The man didn't bother to hide his expression of disgust as he studied the denizens of the bar and watched the scantily clad young girls trying to entice customers to the shabby little bedrooms on the second floor.

Ignoring Lancaster, Hogan watched an Algerian arm-wrestle with a mountainous German. He recognized both men. Alain Dupré was a French colonial who had joined the French Foreign Legion and been shipped to Laos in the 1970s to protect France's interests in Indochina. The French military departure from Southeast Asia left him with no way to use his war-developed skills. So he chose the only form of occupation he could find—hiring himself out to the highest bidder.

Gunther Holzman had been raised in Vientiane by a German missionary couple and had become an adopted member of one of the numerous hill tribes who were constantly warring with the central government to maintain their independence. Since the Communist rebellions, he, too, had become a full-time mercenary.

As a counterinsurgency specialist, Hogan had hired both men for special missions in the past. Not that he trusted them. They were proud to admit that, for a fee, even their own mothers' lives wouldn't be guaranteed. Hogan was glad no one had hired them to dispose of him. Despite their former association, he knew they wouldn't hesitate to accept an assignment to end his life.

He waited for one of them to recognize him. Meanwhile, a crowd had gathered around the wrestlers' table, loudly cheering them on.

The battle between the German and the Algerian was becoming bitter. Black Jack could see Dupré glancing at the dagger tucked into his waistband. It was time to break up the fight before somebody got hurt.

With the hint of a smile on his face, Hogan pushed his chair back and stood up. Nothing had changed since the last time he had been in the White Poppy.

He picked up the water pitcher. Next to him, Lancaster looked surprised. He started to ask a question.

Hogan put a finger to his mouth, then walked over to the arm wrestlers' table. Gently he eased his way through the crowds, lifted the pitcher in the air and emptied its frigid contents on the heads of the two men.

The crowd gasped and waited for a violent reaction from the two seated men.

The straining arms separated suddenly as both men turned to face the source of the ice water. There was fury and hatred in the Algerian's eyes as he yelled, "Who dares...?" Then a big grin crept across his face when he saw Hogan.

"Jackee!" he yelled, slurring Hogan's first name. "I should have known, *mon ami,* that you were not dead," he said, wrapping his huge arms around the American and squeezing.

The German shook his head. "You are still crazy man, friend Hogan. Why did you interrupt our game?"

"It's too hot to arm-wrestle," Jack said, breaking free of the Algerian's hold and grasping the German's outstretched hand.

The Algerian shoved his face up against the scarred face of the German.

"I was ahead," he said with a challenging scowl.

"Ahead?" The German sneered. "Another minute, and your wrist would have hung as limp as that of a froufrou."

The Frenchman clenched his fists and jumped into a brawler's stance. "Are you accusing me of being a faggot?"

The crowds backed away to provide room for the impending fight. Hogan stepped between them.

"I'm buying," he said quietly.

Dupré lowered his hands. "Beer or something stronger?"

"Name your poison."

The German turned his head to the bar. The ancient Laotian who had worked there since the place opened twenty years ago was reading a newspaper.

"Bartender!"

The barman turned and looked at him.

"A bottle of schnapps and—" He turned to the Frenchman.

The Algerian yelled his order. "Two bottles of schnapps—and give the bill to this crazy American."

The bartender nodded and reached under the counter.

The onlookers seemed disappointed that there was no brawl and drifted away from the table. The bartender showed up with two unlabeled quarts and set them down.

Hogan handed him a small stack of Laotian bills, and the bartender retreated.

Lancaster got up and announced he had to go pay a visit to the facilities.

"Take your time," Hogan suggested.

The Bangkok intelligence agent looked worried. "You won't disappear?"

"I'll be right here with my two friends," Black Jack promised.

Hogan waited for Lancaster to walk away. Then asked the Algerian, "What's this about my being dead?"

"The word around the White Poppy was that somebody hired a Cambodian contractor to put you away," the French-accented man explained.

"Hear any reason why he was hired?"

The Algerian shrugged. "Who knows? Perhaps somebody you offended a long time ago. Pom-Pom was giving odds—five to three—against your surviving."

Pom-Pom was the nickname of the ancient bartender. He ran a bookmaking business on the side, betting on the lives of the bar's regulars instead of on sporting events.

"We heard that the contractor was blown away a few days ago," the German added. "Your work?"

Hogan shook his head. "First I heard about him."

Dupré looked incredulous. "You mean no one has taken a shot at you recently?"

Jack Hogan thought back to the attacks in Arizona and the attempt outside Don Muang Airport. "A few local cowboys thought they would try out their toy guns on me a few days ago."

"And what happened to them?"

Hogan shrugged.

The Algerian slapped him across the back, almost knocking Black Jack to the bare wooden floor.

"So why are you here?"

"Business meeting."

A look of surprise crossed Dupré's face. "Are you getting into our business? I thought you were still connected to your government man. I was just going to ask you if you had any assignments for us. Work's been thin around here lately."

"He still is, and no, he hasn't got any assignments to hand out," a soft voice with a Southern accent commented.

The three men turned.

The short, stocky man who stood near their table clenched a long cigar in his mouth. In his off-white linen suit, he looked like a Southern plantation owner. He studied Hogan briefly.

"If you're done socializing, I'd like a word with you."

Hogan pushed his chair out and stood up. Leaning across the table, he grinned at the two mercenaries.

"Got to go. You know, all play and no work makes Jack a poor boy."

He glanced at the expression on the face of the man from Washington. Usually Wilson responded to his remarks with a smile. This time his face was cold and expressionless.

"I just found out who's responsible for Harwood," he said.

17

Dressed in a coarse cassock, a lone figure wandered around the ruins of the long-abandoned monastery trying to control his new feelings. But his eyes betrayed a desperate anger, and when his hood slipped aside, his pale blond hair glimmered in the dimness like a threat.

The large irregular blocks of stone that formed the walls of the huge building irritated him with their asymmetrical appearance. So did the immense boulders that acted as breakers in the waters around the small island.

Even the blue-green sea stretching for miles in every direction was a source of annoyance, an annoyance that was fed by everything around him.

A futile anger was building inside him at the ineptness of the creatures he had selected to assist him in his search.

He had made such careful plans in both worlds. Leasing the island in this world under the pretext of developing it into a resort, and creating a mass exodus heading for the Forbidden Region in the other world under the guise of a religious pilgrimage.

But as before, two creatures were coming between him and his goal. The red-bearded warrior and the equally violent man called Hogan.

They had mocked his power, defied his underlings and acted completely unafraid.

What manner of creatures were they? In the countless worlds he had explored for the life-sustaining glowing rocks, he had never encountered anything like them.

He had taken personal command of the campaign in the other world. The hired soldiers could only be depended on to deal with those who directly opposed him.

And even they had failed when they went up against the ruler of the Kalabrians.

The American general had again promised to rid him of the American who had defied him for so long. This was the military man's last chance. If he failed again, he would lose everything.

Including his life.

MIKHAIL DOESTENTOV gripped the wheel of the ancient leased Mercedes and stared at the tall steel fence surrounding the uranium processing factory as he slowly drove by the entrance. The sign above the large gate read, Pacov Uranium Processing Plant.

The two-lane road was empty. He glanced at his steel wristwatch.

9:00 a.m.

The former Spetsnaz colonel didn't know why his former commander, the now-retired Marshal Vishnikov, wanted explosives with delayed timers around the Czechoslovakian nuclear complex. And he really didn't care.

This had been the first decent-paying assignment the ex-Spetsnaz officer had gotten since he and the team he'd recruited had been discharged from the Soviet army.

They had successfully gotten past the barriers last night and placed packages of explosives inside the processing buildings and around the storage tanks, then set the timers for ten tonight.

He was making his last inspection to ensure no one had discovered the "gifts" they had left last night.

He watched as the guards led the leashed dogs around the grounds, sniffing for unfamiliar odors. One of the team, Daniel Temkin Aperov, had suggested they place the explosives inside paper bags filled with ground coffee to confuse the guard animals. It was a trick, he said, that drug dealers used to smuggle narcotics into the United States.

Mikhail had approved the suggestion and sent Aperov out with some of the small expense fund Vishnikov had given him to make the purchase.

The ex-Spetsnaz officer became tense as he saw a dog pause near where they had buried one of the packages. He relaxed when the large Doberman turned away and continued his inspection elsewhere.

It was time to pick up the rest of the team and drive to Prague. Even though it was not far, the roads from this small Czechoslovakian village to the capital were in desperate need of repair, and the flight that would take them back to Russia was scheduled to leave in three hours.

He drove away from the factory and toward the small inn where the officers were sipping coffee and waiting for his return.

Mikhail was pleased he had not forgotten what he had learned when he was on active duty. Soon, if the marshal was telling the truth, he would be using his talents for his country, rather than having to sell them to unsavory clients in the Middle East.

Doestentov didn't know how the elderly former member of the presidium would accomplish it, but there was something in the way he had made the commitment that raised hope.

"I have met with important friends," Vishnikov had said when they had met at his dacha on the outskirts of Moscow. "Do this for me and you will be rewarded."

The marshal had not been annoyed when Doestentov had pointed out that he had a family to support and could not work for free. Instead, Vishnikov had handed him an envelope filled not with rubles but real American dollars.

He didn't waste time wondering where the marshal had gotten such wealth. There had been more than enough to hire the best of his former Spetsnaz companions, pay for transportation and supplies and give his wife money for rent and food.

The ex-colonel wondered if Vishnikov planned to have the Russian President and his cohorts executed and announce a return to the hard-line style of Communist that existed before *Glasnost*.

It might be the solution to the difficulties that so many Soviets such as himself were facing.

There had been enough complaints from the people about the acceleration of the economic decline that seemed to follow the end of the Cold War. Doestentov and his men were among those who were vocal about their preference for the old-style Russia.

He stopped the car and looked back before he drove around the curve that would place the large factory out of his view.

Many would die before this night ended, but the thought did not bother Doestentov. In the world he understood, life was only a temporary stopping place between birth and death.

And perhaps in a little while he would again be sitting in the rear seat of a large military vehicle ordering his driver to take him home, and not on a narrow two-lane road in a remote part of Czechoslovakia.

18

Black Jack waited for Wilson to speak, but Wilson kept glancing around the bar curiously.

"Nothing really changes in a place like this," the elegantly dressed man commented. "Different faces, same people."

Hogan remembered that it had been in just such a place that he had agreed to work for Wilson after the two of them had emptied a bottle of Jack Daniel's Tennessee Sour Mash.

Hogan leaned forward. "So what do you know?"

"The man we have fingered is James Mattoon Holaday."

Hogan looked shocked. "The air force general?" He shook his head in disbelief. "No way. The man's a national hero."

"We're meeting someone with stories about Holaday you won't believe. But he swears he can prove them."

"Anyone I know?"

"From a long time ago," the Southerner replied cryptically. Then looked up. "Here comes Lancaster."

The agent was looking flustered as he approached the table. "I'm sorry I took so long. There was a young girl—maybe thirteen or fourteen—in the back who said she was in trouble and needed my help."

"And did you?" Wilson asked sarcastically.

"I offered to. She asked if I had twenty dollars for an hour's worth of fun." He looked stunned. "She needed the money to support her children. She was only a child herself."

"They start them young out here," Wilson replied matter-of-factly. "Sit down and order another drink, Howard."

The agent obeyed and ordered another beer.

"So when do we meet our informant?" Hogan prodded.

Wilson looked toward the front door. He saw the uniformed man enter and slowly said, "Right now."

Hogan looked around and immediately recognized General Soong. He made a face as the Laotian pulled out a chair and sat down.

"Hogan," Soong said in a cold, polite voice.

"General Soong." Hogan saw no reason to hide his dislike. "I hear you have a monopoly of agricultural exports from Laos."

"Not quite a monopoly. But close." The Laotian looked at Wilson. "Are you agreeable to my terms?"

Wilson nodded. "We can work out something if the information is worthwhile."

Hogan looked skeptical. "You sure you didn't make up this story about General Holaday?"

"Four planeloads," the general continued, ignoring Hogan's remark.

"Agreed," Wilson said crisply. "And the attacks against Hogan will also cease?"

Soong was silent for a second, then reluctantly nodded. "My unfortunate son shall be waiting for me when I die to blame me for letting him remain dishonored."

Wilson again turned his attention on the Laotian warlord. "Please repeat what you told me."

"I was invited to meet with a number of other retired military officers for private discussions."

"About what?"

"Taking control of our governments."

"By whom?"

The Laotian handed over a photograph he had taken from his office wall. "By this man."

Hogan studied the picture. It showed Soong in uniform standing next to a tall, handsome American air force general. General James Mattoon Holaday.

"Why would he invite you to join?"

"Because we have been business associates since he left Vietnam."

Hogan was eyeing Wilson skeptically. "Do you believe him?"

"Unfortunately yes. I made a call to Washington to verify some of the information he gave me." He shook his head sadly. "It's all true. Like a lot of idols, Holaday has clay feet."

"You haven't given me any details about the others involved or their timetable," Wilson reminded Soong.

"You will have everything—after you have kept your end of the bargain."

Wilson studied the man's inscrutable features. "Will you be a witness against Holaday?"

"Not if it means coming to the United States and facing arrest by your authorities."

Wilson leaned across the table. "Will you sign an affidavit that Holaday was your American distributor and organized the attacks against the nuclear sites?"

"Can you provide the planes and the warehouses?"

Wilson didn't hesitate. "Yes. If the affidavit contains all the details."

"In that case, I will give the signed statement to Hogan."

Wilson gestured to Lancaster to stand up. "Then we can leave." He turned to Hogan. "After you get the affidavit, courier it to me from Bangkok."

"What about Holaday?"

"The Justice Department will deal with him."

Hogan let out all of his anger in one word. "No!"

A number of heads turned in his direction, and he lowered his voice.

"He owes me."

"You have a better way to handle him?"

"The only way."

Wilson pursed his lips and stared at the Cuban cigar in his hand. Then made a decision.

"I don't want to know. Just make it something that can be explained away."

Hogan gave an okay sign. Wilson shrugged and turned to Lancaster.

"Let's get out of here. This is no place for gentle older men like us," he said in his most genteel Southern accent.

Being back in Vientiane after almost ten years meant catching up with old friends—male and female. He had left Dupré and Holzman back at the White Poppy, sleeping off the bottles of whiskey he had bought them.

One of the older regulars at the bar—an attractive young woman called Suzanne—had invited him to spend the night at her place.

But the sweet face of Astrah floated in his mind, and he declined. He went back to his hotel instead, turning Wilson's words over in his mind. Dealing with men like Soong seemed wrong, but it seemed at times that there was no other choice.

He drifted off into an uneasy sleep eventually, dreaming of long flashing knives and rifle shots. He woke up in a sweat, and lay on his bed motionless. Suddenly he had a feeling that he was not alone in the bedroom. The Beretta and the long knife were on the night table next to the bed, and instinctively he reached for them.

"No, *mon ami*. Leave them there."

He recognized the voice. Dupré.

Someone snapped the overhead light on.

Dupré and Holzman were standing at the foot of the bed with automatic pistols in their hands.

Hogan knew why they were there, but not who had sent them. "Why?"

"We got a job after you left the bar."

"So who is your benefactor?"

"I guess it doesn't matter now if you know," Holzman said. "It was Soong."

Black Jack was surprised. Wilson and Soong had made a deal. Free transportation in exchange for an affidavit.

"Did he tell you why?"

Hogan looked past the two mercenaries. He thought he saw a change of light in the room.

"Something about his son's honor being worth more than four planeloads of opium." Dupré shrugged. "Sometimes these Laotians talk in circles."

"Time we got this over with," Holzman said. "I left a fresh bottle on the table at the White Poppy." He glanced at Dupré, who nodded.

"Sorry, *mon ami*. But this is business."

A shot rang out, shattering the silence with its reverberations. Dupré looked surprised as he fell forward on the bed. The wound in his back began to stain the bed covers a deep red.

Holzman turned in the direction of the shot, and Hogan grabbed the long knife by the tip of the blade and threw it.

The tip of the blade slid into the small of the back with deadly effect.

Holzman turned with a vacant stare, then slid to the floor.

Black Jack looked toward the doorway. A young officer in uniform stood in a sliver of light, a .45 still gripped in his right hand.

"Now we are even," he said.

Hogan slid out from under the covers and walked around the bodies to where the officer was standing.

He was confused. "Even?"

"I am a Hmong."

"I know your people well."

"Especially my honored uncle."

The former Green Beret noncom wasn't sure who the uniformed officer meant. He had fought alongside hundreds of the Hmong.

"You aided my uncle and his wives to relocate to a place called Fresno, California, when the war ended. If you hadn't, the central government and the Communist Pathet Lao would have killed him."

Now Hogan remembered the uncle's name. "Vang."

"Exactly. And at last our family's debt is repaid."

He started backing out, but Hogan stopped him with a question. "What about Soong and his affidavit?"

"Unfortunately neither is available."

Hogan retrieved his long knife from the German mercenary's body and wiped it on the bed cover.

"I could try to convince him," he said coldly.

"He is beyond convincing. He has gone to join his son and explain why his honor will never be redeemed."

"And who takes over his business?"

For the first time the young officer smiled. "I do, of course."

Hogan remembered Wilson's comment. Nothing really changes. New faces. Same people.

A new warlord had just been born.

19

Father Vigilante looked impatient.

"Where are the others?"

Holaday had just arrived by private plane from the mainland. He explained that it took time for some of the others in the group to arrange for transportation to the island. But his words didn't seem to penetrate.

He had postponed his television speech for a week, but he was as anxious as the multimillionaire who was backing him to get the meeting going. A whole country to command was waiting for his return.

He wondered why the recluse looked so wan. It was as if his strength had been drained by the strain of helping Holaday put together the plans. The general was sympathetic. The wealthy young man was not used to the pressures of warfare. That was why Holaday had been asked to take charge and run the show.

"Will Soong come?"

Holaday had decided not to invite him. He was still bitter about the demands Soong had made.

"No. But he'll follow orders." He checked the list of invitees. "The Russian will be here. And the South African general."

"Good," the man in monk's robes said softly.

"Also the general from Brazil and the man we recruited from India. Lew Hazelford from the United Nations will get in tonight. The others said they were trying to make travel arrangements."

"Then by tomorrow morning we should have a good representation of the group."

"I hope the conference won't take too long."

The hermit smiled weakly. "No. You will be back in your country in more than enough time to prepare for your television speech."

Holaday was again amazed. How did Vigilante know what he had been thinking?

WILSON WAS LISTENING to Black Jack relate Soong's death. His hand tightened on the receiver as Hogan went on. "Affidavit or no affidavit, I'm heading for Holaday's ranch."

But Wilson had already done some checking on the whereabouts of the retired air force general. "You won't find him there. I checked, and he took a flight for Greece yesterday."

"Where to?"

"He rented a private plane to fly him to some small island. Perhaps he got a tip that Soong had turned on him. But he can't stay in hiding forever. Eventually he's going to want to come back to the United States."

Hogan sounded irritated. "I can't wait for him to make up his mind. Maybe I'll head for the island."

Just then Mrs. Bolivar entered Wilson's office. "Hold on a second," he said into the phone. He turned to his secretary impatiently. "What is it?"

"Valerie Wilding is on the phone."

"I'll have to call her back."

"She sounded frightened and said she had information on a General James Holaday she thought you'd want."

Wilson's eyes flickered. He turned back to the telephone.

"Stay where you are. I may have what we've been looking for on the other line. I'll call you back."

HOGAN BOARDED a flight to Singapore and from there caught a nonstop flight to Hawaii. From Honolulu he flew to Seattle, then loudly asked at the ticket counter about the next nonstop to Washington, D.C.

But at the last minute he purchased a coach ticket to Minneapolis. Then he called Wilson to say he was on his way and got the last seat on the next flight to Washington.

The White House aide had offered to send someone to pick him up at Washington National Airport, but Hogan refused. He'd find his own transportation to the hunting lodge in Virginia where Valerie Wilding had been secreted away. Then he'd see what useful information she had to reveal.

The flight from Minneapolis landed at Washington National Airport on time. The crowded plane disgorged its cargo of passengers, who wandered down the narrow lower-level walkways until they came to the flight of stairs that led up to the lobby.

Black Jack Hogan lugged his worn khaki-colored raincoat and sandwiched himself between a group of executives. He pretended to be part of the group. He feigned interest as the five men and women talked incessantly in an almost-gibberish language about gigabytes and multifile servers, but he was on the alert.

It had been a long, complicated flight, and all Hogan wanted was to get to his destination, take a bath and catch a quick nap before he and Wilson got down to details.

As he walked toward the baggage claim area to retrieve his small suitcase, he heard a voice call his name.

"Hogan. John Hogan."

He turned and saw a familiar-looking bald man in an immaculate business suit moving toward him.

Hogan tried to put the face with a name, but the connection kept eluding him.

"I thought you'd still be in Arizona visiting your family," the bald man said nervously.

Hogan realized who he was. The senior medical officer at Walter Reed Hospital who had supervised his annual physical.

"Just passing through, Dr. Martingdale," Black Jack said, trying to sound casual. "I'm still on vacation."

"I'm just starting mine. Where are you heading this time?"

Hogan thought quickly. "The Shenandoah Valley. I've always wanted to hear the mountain people sing in their native habitat, instead of in some concert hall."

The colonel forced a grin on his face. "Talk about small worlds. I'm heading to a medical conference down there. How are you traveling?"

"I'm going to rent a car," Black Jack said hastily.

Shoving his arm under Hogan's, the army doctor dragged him down a corridor toward a remote gate.

"Nonsense. I've been able to con a helicopter from the air force. After all we put you through last week, you deserve the luxury of a free flight."

As he struggled in his mind to find a way to reject the offer, Hogan wished he had been able to find a way to carry his automatic and long knife through the airport security checks.

BECKER WAS GOING to be in charge and on the spot this time. He waited around the motel in Alexandria, Virginia, for the call from the air force helicopter pilot he had recruited. He had made a last-minute decision to fly here and make sure that nothing went wrong for once.

The flight with Hogan was scheduled to leave Washington National Airport an hour ago. The pilot should have called—unless something had gone wrong.

Everything that could had already gone wrong, the grizzly-faced ex-Special Forces noncom reminded himself. It was about time he thought about bailing out.

Holaday was getting on his nerves. It had been different when the old man just ran the distribution business for Soong. But since he'd decided to get involved in politics, his demands had become more and more outrageous.

Having someone killed for cheating or for reneging on paying their monthly protection fees was one thing. But murdering thousands of people just to make a point was insane.

It wasn't even the number of deaths that bothered him. What got him mad was that there didn't seem to be a practical reason for killing them.

But what proved most worrisome was the thought that Valerie Wilding may have already gotten to the federal authorities with the information she had on their operation.

The only thing that gave him any hope was the certainty that the brunette would not talk to anyone she didn't trust. Valerie was too smart to sentence herself to a long prison term on a drug-dealing charge.

After Hogan had been eliminated, Becker would have to do something about the next man up, Wilson. That would close the doors for Holaday's former mistress.

He called his ex-Special Forces contact.

"Hear anything about the helicopter flight?"

"Not a word. I checked with some buddies in the control tower. They said it took off late."

"Any chance it could have crashed?"

"Maybe. Check me later."

Whether Hogan was dead or not, there was still Wilson. Becker decided to go after him rather than sit around a motel room and do nothing.

Sitting down at the small desk in his room, he doodled on a sheet of paper with the motel-furnished pen while he worked out a plan in his head.

Think of this as a mission, he told himself. You know the target and where he is. Can you handle it alone, or do you need manpower?

He looked up and studied his image in the mirror over the desk.

"You need men," he told his reflection.

Then he made a list of eight men. Siminov and Rubianka had been with the KGB until the recent reforms in Russia. Drescher and Moechelberg had worked undercover for the Stasi in East Germany before the reunification of the two Germanys. Al Marblehead had made it out of Vietnam alive, but holding a dishonorable discharge for his part in a murder-for-hire ring in Saigon. His roommate, Nick Lokens, had spent two years in an army psycho ward when his commanding officer discovered his secret cache of North Vietnamese ears kept hidden in a large jar of pickling juice as mementos of his successful duels with the enemy.

Then there was Ruben Malaguay, who had worked as an enforcer for the Cali drug syndicate. The final recruit was an international competition-grade marksman. Souvanna Minh had been a military attaché in the Washington embassy of the South Vietnamese government until the fall of Saigon. Since then, he had supported his family, both in the United States and in Indochina, by signing on as a mercenary.

With eight men like that, Becker knew he could wipe out Wilson and whatever backup men he had.

Checking the map of Virginia he had purchased at Washington National Airport, Becker decided it would be better strategy to fly his team and their gear into the small airport at Front Royal, rent a pair of four-wheel-drive vehicles and drive the rest of the way than to fly by helicopter to the hunting lodge.

In a few hours all the arrangements had been completed, and it was time to leave.

Becker checked the equipment he had purchased from local connections. The CAR-15 was a perfect sniper weapon. He'd also bought a dozen 30-round clips for it.

The .357 Magnum Smith & Wesson automatic he fondled had more than enough kill power to stop even someone wearing a Kevlar vest.

The prize of his armory was the tubelike rocket launcher he had demanded and the four rockets he'd bought with it. Properly aimed, the weapon could destroy a well-entrenched battery unit. Becker was sure it wouldn't fail against a flimsy wood-frame lodge.

20

Hogan glanced out of his window and up at the Bell helicopter blades that whirled above him in a monotonous pattern.

"Something special going on where you're heading?"

The question came from the copilot, an eager young lieutenant named Dick Haakon.

Hogan didn't answer. The copilot should have known better than to ask questions.

The other air force jockey up front turned and saw the annoyed expression on their passenger's face, then straightened around and looked at his copilot. "Dick, pay attention to the instruments," Captain Peter Harmel said in reprimand.

Haakon gave the pilot a dirty look and lapsed into silence.

Black Jack looked out of the window at the land below him. The ground was a regular pattern and light and dark green, broken occasionally by stands of trees. In the distance were the rises of land and trees that marked the mountains of Virginia and its neighboring states.

Hogan looked everywhere except to his right, where the bald medical officer sat and continued to babble.

In the past hour all he'd heard was a chattering stream of complaints.

Fed up, Black Jack was about to face the good doctor and tell him to ease up. Then he saw that his companion's back was turned to him.

The small man was hunched over. For a moment Hogan wondered if he had gotten sick. Then he leaned over and saw something disappearing into the doctor's pocket. It looked like a syringe.

It occurred to Hogan that the man was diabetic, but he caught a glimpse of the glazed expression on the other's face. He had seen that look before—mostly on drug addicts who spun out their miserable existence on the streets of Phnom Penh and Bangkok.

Dr. Martingdale was a junkie.

The thought sickened Hogan. He leaned his head back against his seat and closed his eyes. There was nothing he could do to stop the man from ruining his life. He had tried in vain too many times with friends back in Vietnam.

He felt a nudge against his side and kept his eyes closed. Now that he was high, the doctor obviously wanted to continue babbling.

There was another nudge. Hogan started getting annoyed. He thought he had made it obvious he was in no mood to listen to any more drug-induced complaints.

He opened his eyes and saw the .45 ACP Colt Commander shoved against his chest.

The man holding the gun grinned at him from his seat in front, then glanced at the doctor.

"Hey, doc, save a little of that shit for me," the copilot cracked.

Hogan knew the odds were bad, but delaying action wouldn't help. With a lightning-fast move he grabbed for the armed man's wrist. They tottered back and forth in the struggle as the alarmed pilot tried to keep the helicopter level with the ground.

"Fire that gun, and we all die," Black Jack grunted.

"No way. I got this baby loaded with soft-noses. Won't damage the government property around us," he snarled as he tried to yank the gun from Hogan's desperate grip.

"You're bluffing."

Glancing quickly to the right, the copilot called for help. "Hey, doc, knock him out with something quick."

The doctor reached down and nervously rummaged through the small medical bag at his feet. He came up holding a filled syringe and turned toward Hogan.

Black Jack made a decision. If he was wrong, he and the others might be dead. But if he didn't do anything, he'd be dead anyway.

He jammed his finger inside the trigger guard of the automatic and shoved it back.

The gun went off, and the slug found a target. Stunned, Martingdale stared at the large bleeding hole that had suddenly appeared in his chest, then slumped forward.

The enraged copilot ripped the automatic free and swung it around.

Hogan quickly hauled the doctor's bleeding body in front of him just as the copilot pulled the trigger.

The second bullet cored into the dead man's head. Before a third round could be fired, Hogan dropped the body and chopped the callused edge of his right hand at the carotid nerve of the copilot.

The armed man let the handgun slide from his grip and stared at Black Jack in shock, then went slack against the pilot.

"At least you weren't bluffing," Hogan told the dead copilot softly.

As the pilot struggled to right the helicopter, Hogan scooped up the fallen weapon and held it against the back of his head.

"Let's take it nice and easy to our destination," he said slowly. "Then we can have a long talk about who set this up."

BLACK JACK WASN'T SURE if he was disgusted or angry as Valerie Wilding described her involvement in the retired air force general's post-military business. Though clearly frightened, the attractive brunette still had an air of confidence, suggesting that she had hopes of extricating herself from the mess.

"It wasn't as though the drugs we imported were sold to people who hadn't used them before. If they didn't buy from our people, they would have just gone out and found another source."

Hogan thought of the thousands of hopelessly addicted children he had seen on the streets of Indochina and was about to snap a bitter reply when Wilson jumped in.

"I appreciate your honesty, Val. But you said you knew something about Harwood."

She looked confused for a moment, then suddenly got a too-wise look on her face.

"What about immunity from the drug charges if I tell you what I know?"

Wilson shook his head. "I can't guarantee that. But I can promise you nobody will be able to find you if you cooperate—about *everything*."

Valerie sighed deeply, then began to speak in a quiet voice.

"Jim—" she turned to Hogan "—General Holaday," she explained, then continued. "Jim and I were in Washington having dinner with this strange-looking millionaire who dressed like a monk, even though he said he wasn't one. The two of them kept talking about how the governments were letting the anarchists and terrorists run their countries and that they had to be stopped before the whole world went crazy."

She looked up. "You understand, Hiram, don't you?"

Wilson smiled and nodded. "Go on, Val."

"Well, this hermit—he went by the name Father Vigilante—said it was up to people like Jim to do something. If Jim was interested, he had some ideas on how it could be done."

Black Jack became impatient. "What's this got to do with Harwood?"

Wilson gave him an icy stare, and Hogan shut up.

"Jim flew to some island off the coast of Greece to meet with the rich man. He lived in some old monastery. When he got back, Jim had Becker—"

Wilson interrupted. "Arnold Becker?"

"Yes, he's worked for Jim ever since Vietnam." She lit a cigarette and inhaled, then let the smoke curl from her mouth. "So he had Becker contact some men he knew."

Hogan jumped in. "What kind of men?"

"The only kind Becker knows. Mercenaries," she replied coolly. "He had a job for them. I wasn't interested, so I didn't bother listening."

Wilson shook his head. "How do you know it has anything to do with Harwood?"

"Because after the meeting, I heard Becker telling Jim they would need his help to get into the plant at Harwood."

She stood up. "Where's the bathroom?"

Wilson pointed to a nearby corridor. "At the very end."

Hogan watched the woman walk away, then asked, "How do you know she won't try to leave?"

"There's no place for her to go. She knows someone is trying to kill her." He smiled. "Besides, I've got two men armed to the gills outside just waiting to get some target practice on anything that moves."

Wilson got to his feet and paced around restlessly.

"A retired war hero hires mercenaries to get rid of a nuclear processing plant in Harwood. It makes no sense."

"None of this does," Black Jack agreed. "And why send a message to the United Nations telling them he's going to keep on doing it until they stop all nuclear production?"

"It would almost make some sense if he owned a lot of petroleum and couldn't get rid of it. But your reports say his only income is from his retirement checks."

"And the income from Soong," Wilson added in a flat tone.

Jack Hogan muttered a question to himself. "What's in it for him?"

Valerie Wilding had just returned and heard the last few words. "Perhaps the weird rich man got Jim to convert to some insane religion that hates nuclear power," the woman suggested.

Hogan turned. His expression reflected his skepticism. "I've heard of some weird religions, but none that thought that nuclear power had something to do with the devil." He pondered for a minute. "I'd like to know what that rich man looks like."

"I can tell you."

Valerie Wilding paused while she poured herself a cup of coffee.

"He had bright yellow hair and the weirdest eyes you ever saw. Looking at his eyes, you'd swear he was Oriental, but he wasn't."

A look of recognition passed across Hogan's face. Now he had an idea. He'd heard just such a man described before, though never seen him.

Wilson saw his expression and asked, "Something wrong?"

"Yeah, but I don't know how to describe it. What's happening, I think, is the beginning of an attempt to take over the world."

Wilson stared at Hogan in silence, as though trying to gauge his mental stability, then heard a gasp from the woman.

She looked shocked, as if Hogan had hit on a nerve.

"That must have been what Jim was hinting about. He kept saying that he and the others were going to get the world straightened out finally."

Wilson jumped in. "Who were the others, Val?"

She started giving names. Hogan could see Wilson's stunned expression as she kept naming some of the most important military leaders in the world.

But Wilson was still trying to deny the possibility. "Somebody's gone crazy thinking they can pull it off. They'll never get past first base—"

The ringing phone interrupted his comment, and he pounced on the telephone. "Wilson."

He recognized the voice on the other end and listened.

"When did this happen, sir? Yes, he's with me now. I'll tell him. Thank you for letting me know, sir." Gently he replaced the receiver in its cradle.

"That was the President," he said to Hogan. "He wanted you to know he's called off the investigation of your involvement in the Bangkok airport incident."

Hogan looked blank. "What investigation?"

"We'll go over it another time," Wilson said impatiently. "What was it you just said about taking over the whole world?"

"I said it might be the beginning of an attempt. And you said they'd never get past first base."

"They're on second base now," the stunned White House aide reported. "A town named Pacov in Czechoslovakia was totally decimated last night when explosions ripped through the local nuclear processing plant. They don't know how many people died. The area is still too hot."

The brunette put a hand to her mouth in dismay. "That was one of the places I heard Jim mention."

Wilson dropped his mask of gentility and grabbed her shoulders. "What were the others, Val?"

She started naming places in Romania, Germany, Russia and South Africa. "I can't remember if there were more," she said nervously. Then she clasped her hands together and turned to the two men. "I can't believe this. Jim Holaday did a lot of rotten things, but he'd never kill innocent people."

"Tell that to Charley Grisolm and his family," Hogan replied frigidly.

She looked at him. "Who are they?"

"They died at Harwood—on the orders of General Holaday."

21

Becker and his team had waited until dusk to move in on the secluded hunting lodge. He'd confirmed that Hogan was still alive and at the hunting lodge.

Luckily both the doctor and the copilot were dead. So his identity was still safe.

He looked up at the sky and saw the clouds blocking out the moon and stars. It was looking like the perfect night for an assault. He looked at the eight men he'd recruited. They were all dressed in camouflage.

He signaled them to gather around him.

"Everybody ready?"

The eight men nodded.

"Check your weapons and make sure."

There were a series of soft clicks as handguns and automatic rifles were inspected.

Becker handed out the tubelike rocket launcher. "Ruben, carry this for me," he said. Next he dealt with the two heavyset Russians, handing them several of the rockets. They were to make the rockets available at the right moment.

He reviewed the attack plan.

Still speaking softly, he held the paper on which he had drawn a crude map after scouting the area earlier.

"The hunting lodge sits on the edge of a plateau about two hundred yards up the road from us. A wired fence surrounds the property. The only entrance is through the main gate.

"My guess is that there's probably one or two armed men guarding it."

Al Marblehead, one of the Americans on the team, asked, "How do we take them out?"

"I'll tell you in a moment. Our targets are in this building," he continued, "which sits about thirty yards from the gate."

"How many in the house?" Drescher demanded.

"The two targets and probably another guard. One of the targets is an older man. It's the other one who's dangerous."

He looked around at the men staring at him. "Anyone hear of John Hogan?"

"Black Jack Hogan?" The question came from Herman Moechelberg. "*Ja,* I have heard about him."

"That's his nickname."

"A bad-news dude," Marblehead commented sourly. "I've heard stories of him taking out five men by himself."

"There are *nine* of us and only one of him," Becker reminded him.

"This is no time to argue," Leo Siminov, former KGB, said bluntly. Then looked at Becker. "You were going to tell us about the gate."

"No problem," Becker assured him. "The whole fence, including the gate, is wired to set off an alarm if someone penetrates it. So we string a wire from one gatepost to the other to fool the system, then use the pipe cutters and snap the chain that's holding the gate shut."

He glanced at the team members. "Any other questions?"

Nobody said a word.

Becker picked up the bag full of tools and slung it over one shoulder, then hefted the CAR-15 in his other hand and started moving toward the gate.

Suddenly he stopped and turned to the Vietnamese mercenary.

"As for Black Jack, it would be safest if you threw a wire around his neck and choked him to death."

Grinning at the prospect, the man took out a length of fine piano wire from his pocket and wrapped it around both of his knuckles.

BROM SAT beside the small fire and watched the meat turn a sizzling brown over it.

The night air in the high plains was chilly and he had pulled his robe around him. Even his stallion had moved closer to the fire so that it could stay warm.

A small object slithered by. The red-bearded warrior glanced at it in disgust. A Galik. The slimy poisonous serpents preferred to come out at night and hunt for their food.

He reached for his broadsword and flicked it away.

Overhead the sky was filled with stars. He could see the twin moons shining brightly down on him.

It wouldn't be so bad if Mora were at his side. But she was back in Tella. Perhaps he had been foolhardy to set out alone to catch up with Zhuzak and the troops. But trying to run a country without Mondlock's help was too much for him.

He was a warrior—a fighter of fights, a leader in battles, and not a wise man who could solve each dispute fairly.

He thought of his cousin, Sola, son of his late uncle, Draka, who had died in the recapturing of Tella from the hordes who had enslaved it. Sola was his age and had been away since childhood, studying in Leanad, the city of Knowers.

Mondlock had gotten him an appointment to join the elite group of men who spent their waking hours learning.

Even if Mondlock was still alive, he was getting old. He needed a helper. If Sola was here, he could sit by their side and help make the decisions of government.

Perhaps, after he had slain the prophet, he would send a messenger to Leanad to petition Sola to return.

Satisfied with his decision, Brom turned the roasting animal flesh again, then opened his water gourd and poured some liquid in the metal cup he had carried.

He lifted it to his mouth, then saw a flicker in it. There was an image of something in the water.

He moved the cup closer to the fire and gazed at the reflection in the light.

It was Hogan.

He was on top of a mountain, holding one of his fire-sticks. Behind him was a white-haired man holding a smaller fire-stick.

Brom smiled.

The long, boring journey to the Forbidden Region where Zhuzak and his men were heading would soon be interrupted.

He gathered up his weapons and waited.

VALERIE HAD PREPARED a simple dinner, anxious to be doing something.

She put the steaks she had found in the freezer on the broiler and started boiling water for the vegetables when she heard shots from the grounds. Turning off the oven, she ran into the living room.

Hiram Wilson and Hogan were already racing to the door. Both were armed.

Wilson gripped a 9 mm H&K automatic in his right hand. Hogan had the M-16A slung over his shoulder and was strapping a webbed belt around his middle with one hand while he gripped a handful of filled clips with his other. The holster that hung from it carried a 9 mm Beretta 91F. Two of the grenades Wilson had brought with him were hanging from loops, and a strange-handled knife was shoved inside the belt.

Wilson stopped and looked at the woman.

"Stay inside and keep low."

Filled with sudden panic, she started looking around for a hiding place, then saw the canvas bag.

Inside it were a lot of filled clips, hand grenades and a 9 mm Beretta.

Better to die fighting than to be found and murdered, she decided. Besides, maybe Jim had come himself. Then she could show him how wrong he'd been to kick her out.

She grabbed the automatic and two clips, then headed for the window when a burst of lead shattered the pane of glass. She let the automatic fall from her hand and dived behind a couch.

HOGAN SAW barely discernible shadows move between the low pines toward the house. From below, near the front gate, he heard another burst of fire and the screams of a dying man.

The guards have been taken out, he thought, and crept forward.

One of the shadows darted out from a cluster of trees and ran for a low clump of shrubs.

Hogan let loose a trio of 5.56 mm rounds at the center of the bushes. He heard a quick yelp but was in no position to follow up.

Hot slugs winged through the air to his left, and Hogan dived onto the ground. He rolled to the trunk of an evergreen, then sat up and washed the open area in front of him with death-seekers from his M-16A.

A second voice reacted with a howl as the hungry pieces of lead found a lodging place.

Suddenly there was deadly silence. All movement had stopped.

Hogan cocked his head, trying to guess what the attackers' next move would be. At this point, the silence signaled greater danger.

Then a familiar voice whispered, "Where the hell are you, Black Jack?"

Hogan spun his head around and saw Wilson clearly framed in the light from inside the lodge. He was holding an automatic in his right hand.

"Get down," he shouted, scurrying furiously to his left as he snapped the order.

Wilson looked startled, then started to move into the dark lawn when a burst exploded from beyond the second tier of shrubs.

Stunned, Wilson stared into the night wildly, then slumped to the ground.

Hogan wanted to go over to see if he was still alive. But that would only provide two dead bodies. Instead, he moved softly into the woods.

Gunfire would only attract gunfire. He slung the automatic rifle over his shoulder and whipped out the Kalabrian long knife.

Moving with the stealth of his forefathers, he peered into the dark and made out a bulky figure hiding in the shadow of a tree.

Moving quietly behind him, Hogan tapped the armed man on the shoulder. Then, as the man turned to see what had touched him, Black Jack quickly slit his throat from ear to ear.

Clamping a hand over the dying man's mouth, he held it there until the head fell forward, then let the body slide to the ground.

Stealthily Hogan moved into deeper shadows.

22

Even though the two guards at the gate were dead, Becker knew he had to move quickly. Jack Hogan was an experienced jungle fighter like himself.

Marblehead was at his side.

"Check and see who's missing," Becker ordered in a whisper.

The mercenary slipped into the dark. Within a few minutes he returned. "Three gone. The fat Russian, one of the Germans and Nick Lokens."

"That leaves six of us and two of them."

"Only one," Marblehead corrected him. "I took the white-haired guy down."

Becker was pleased. Half the mission was accomplished. The white-haired man must have been Hogan's boss, Hiram Wilson.

Getting Hogan would be more difficult. He saw the rocket launcher being dragged and gestured for Ruben to join him.

"Ruben, get that tube on your shoulder."

Marblehead vanished and returned with one of the 2.75 inch rockets.

The Colombian lifted the rocket launcher and carefully balanced it on his shoulder while Becker fitted the shell into the tube.

Becker pointed to an area near a stand of evergreens to the left of the lodge.

"Take it over there and aim for the front of the building," he ordered.

Ruben focused through the sighting device on the side of the launcher.

"Hogan ain't in there," Marblehead reminded the man who'd hired him.

"I know, but I don't want him sneaking back in and making a call for help."

HOGAN WATCHED the mercenary move with the launcher. The woman was still inside, and he was determined to bring her back to testify against the general.

He reached down to touch the two grenades dangling from his webbed belt. It was too dark to see which was the incendiary and which the fragmentation grenade. He grabbed one and, hoping it was the fragmentation missile, pulled the pin, started counting and then released it with an underhand pitch.

He saw the flames shoot high into the sky and knew he'd been wrong. Screams of pain tore from the mouth of the stocky man who had been holding the launcher on his shoulder as the flames enveloped him in an inferno of death.

Dropping the tube, the mercenary threw himself around on the ground trying to smother the flames and kill the agony of his burns. The contents of the incendiary grenade had spread over a five-foot area. Trees and shrubs were set on fire all around the body, making it impossible to retrieve the launcher.

Black Jack had raced across the ground before the grenade made contact. From the pattern of resumed firing, he could tell the enemy had fanned out to catch him in a closing circle.

A noise from behind made him swivel around. He saw the grinning face of the ex-Special Forces non-com holding a government-issue Colt automatic at his head.

"You got a reputation for getting out of scrapes, Hogan," Becker said with a harsh laugh. "Until now."

Even as Hogan considered throwing himself side-ways, a figure loomed behind his executioner.

A naked blade carved through the empty air and came down through Becker's shoulder and chest, cut-ting a deadly path through his vital organs.

Brom lowered his sword. "That's done."

"We've got four left," Black Jack warned.

"An uneven fight."

But Hogan knew Brom wasn't complaining.

"Then let's get rid of them.

THE REMAINING RUSSIAN, Siminov, teamed up with the German. Together they moved cautiously through a wooded area.

Moechelberg was frustrated. "Where could the swine have run?"

The answer came almost immediately when Brom ran his blade through the questioning man's back. Stunned, the German turned and looked as if he was staring at a specter. Never before had he seen a crim-son-haired giant who dressed like a barbarian and used a sword, except in movies.

Suddenly another idea flashed through his mind—his last thought. I've never died before, he thought in astonishment.

Then, heaving blood from his punctured lungs and heart, the mercenary fell forward.

The Russian had sensed the movement behind him. He spun around and recognized one of the figures from Becker's description. It was Hogan. Swinging his AK-47, he tried to get off a round, but the strange-looking long knife the American held slid down his neck and out the back of his neck before he could.

Gagging in an effort to cough up the surgically sharp blade from his throat, the Russian tried to fire the automatic rifle. But his trigger finger wouldn't obey his command.

He looked puzzled, then a fog covered his eyes, and he saw nothing but the hell he had entered.

Hogan freed his blade and quickly wiped it as Brom watched and shook his head, lifting his broadsword from the skewered body.

"You still have the strange habit of cleansing yourself from the blood of your enemies," he commented. "I wonder how your gods ever know that you are a great warrior."

"We can argue about that later," Black Jack said. "There are at least two more killers out there."

MARBLEHEAD RAN into the Vietnamese in the dark. He had almost shot at the slim figure but at last realized who it was.

"From what I can figure, everyone's gone but us. Maybe it's time we split."

"Yes," the Vietnamese agreed.

"No," a new voice said.

The two mercenaries turned to the sound. Hogan and Brom stood a few feet away from them. Brom had sheathed his sword and was holding the automatic rifle he'd taken from the skewered assassin. Hogan held the M-16A in front of him.

Marblehead thought quickly. He looked at the counterinsurgency specialist and his huge fighting companion.

"Hey, why don't we just get out of here and call it quits?" But his hand was sliding toward his belt for a handgun.

Hogan and the Kalabrian glanced at each other. The mercenary took advantage of the momentary distraction and brought up his AK-47. He started to squeeze the trigger when Brom, holding the retrieved weapon in his hands like a shovel, began to fire.

The stunned mercenary's body spun around from impact of the 5.56 mm lead until a loud click announced that the clip was empty.

The Vietnamese rushed at Hogan and feinted a blow to his wrist, then attempted to crush his windpipe with an expert slash. Hogan twisted out of his assailant's path and whipped a booted foot at his kneecap.

Despite the searing pain, the man wasn't about to give up. Instead, he whipped out a small dagger he wore in a sheath around his wrist and threw himself forward.

Hogan grabbed the wrist of the blade-bearing hand and desperately twisted until the dagger fell to the ground. The man pretended to surrender, then twisted his body and kicked out, letting his bony toe connect with Hogan's side.

The sharp point struck where the American had recently been wounded. Hogan winced, then grabbed the ankle and twisted. Expertly the Vietnamese allowed himself to be turned, then loosened his body to free himself and dropped to the ground, immediately going into a forward roll.

Bouncing to his feet, he brought the callused edge of his right hand up and chopped at Hogan's carotid with a hard slash. The American waited until the blow almost landed and tripped the attacker with a leg block.

As Minh sprawled on the ground, Hogan fell on top of him and rammed a hand just under the rib cage. The Vietnamese tried to wriggle away, but the large man kept him pinned down.

Black Jack's fingers pressed up until they found what they were seeking. He could feel the throbbing muscle that kept blood pumping through the Vietnamese's body.

His hardened fingers assaulted the muscle again and again as the man fought to free himself. The Vietnamese managed to free a hand and slashed it at Hogan's nose.

Bone cracked, and blood ran into Hogan's mouth, but he continued to pound the protesting muscle again and again, until the organ quit and, with a last shudder, the thin man stopped struggling.

Exhausted from the effort, Hogan clambered to his feet.

"You must teach me how to do that," Brom said with admiration. "You fight as well without a weapon as you do with one."

"It takes time to learn."

"Then we will make the time."

Hogan sprinted back toward the building with Brom right behind him.

Wilson was lying where he'd fallen. Hogan knelt at his side to examine him. There was an ugly red groove on the side of his head, but Hogan could find no other wounds.

He checked the pulse. It was weak but present.

Brom looked down at the still form. "Who is he?"

"His name is Wilson."

"*The* Wilson?"

At Hogan's nod, the Kalabrian looked astounded. "This is your king?"

"Sometimes he thinks he is."

"He's very puny and old."

"But quite important."

Brom shook his head. "He wouldn't survive a day in Kalabria," he said as he proceeded up the stairs into the lodge.

"You'd be surprised," Hogan called out as he followed him.

They found the body of Valerie Wilding near the couch. Apparently she'd been firing through the window, and two bullets had found their way into her torso. Hogan stood looking down at her, shaking his head.

Brom studied the expression on his face. "Was she one of your women?"

"No. She has her own sins, but the man she was running away from is trying to destroy our world."

"Like this prophet is my world."

Black Jack was tempted to tell the alien warrior that the prophet and the man behind Holaday were probably the same. But he knew the Kalabrian would consider him mad. Even he wasn't sure of his sanity when he thought about it.

Brom looked at his brother-in-arms. "I was on my way to the Forbidden Region. I think that is where the prophet is holding Mondlock prisoner. I could use your help."

The American was thinking of General Holaday as he replied, "There's something I must do here first."

"Come soon, Hogan." Then Brom stepped forward and vanished.

THE EMBERS of the small fire were cold by the time Brom was transported back to his campsite. The large stallion looked at him curiously. If he didn't know better, Brom could have sworn the animal wanted to ask where he'd been.

How could he tell him—or anyone—when he didn't know. It was another world. Different than the world he knew so well, and cluttered with strange objects whose uses Brom couldn't comprehend, except for the fire-sticks. But it was a world populated by people just like this one.

Especially Hogan.

The Kalabrian leader kicked sand over the few smoking chars of wood, then packed his belongings and mounted the animal. He pressed the horse on as night started to recede, and finally he spotted the enemy.

From the top of a hill he could see armed men engaged in battle. Even from this distance—hours away on horseback—Brom could identify the Kalabrians by their armor. Swords flashed in the dim light of dawn, as did the metal edges of flying axes and spears. He could hear the yells of fighting men and the frightened protests of their animals. He spurred his horse and charged ahead, moving down the hill in a blur, his red hair like a flag in the wind.

CAPTAIN ZHUZAK guided his mount into the midst of the enemy and slashed his wide sword at the neck of their leader. The weapon found its mark, and fountains of pulsating blood spurted from severed vessels as he pulled back his weapon and drove it through the man's leather armor.

The suddenly lifeless form fell from his horse. Captain Zhuzak jumped to the ground and quickly separated the fallen man's head from his body, then speared it on the tip of his sword and held it high for everyone to see.

The enemy horsemen saw the head of their leader bob in the air. It was a bad omen for them all. Looking at one another, they turned their animals and raced away from the fight.

Some of the Kalabrians set off in hot pursuit.

"Let them go," the captain shouted loudly. "Just keep one for questioning."

He surveyed the large flat field around him. The bodies of the fallen enemy seemed to be piled on top of one another. Here and there he spotted the armor of a Kalabrian warrior.

After the battle he would send men to summon the funeral preparers. They would dress the bodies and prepare them for the ceremonial fires so that Pavad, the god of the dead, could escort them to their final homes.

Two of his men rode up, dangling a terrified youth between them. He was still wearing his armor.

"This one tried to hide under a dead horse," one of the warriors announced.

"Let him down," Zhuzak ordered.

The soldiers opened their hands. The frightened boy fell to the ground, then got on his knees and crawled to the black-bearded captain.

"If you want to live," Zhuzak told him loudly, "tell us where you were all going." He allowed his horse a few prancing steps and swished his sword in the air to hurry the prisoner.

Then Zhuzak spotted Lord Brom picking his way through the battleground. Zhuzak waved his sword, and the Kalabrian leader rode up to his side.

"Welcome, Lord Brom. We're just taking care of our dead, but there were more of the enemy who lost their lives. The rest retreated."

Brom looked around at the carnage. "So I see." He turned and stared at the captive. "Who is he?"

"A storyteller. He's been telling us what's been going on at the edge of the Forbidden Region and where this force was going." He lifted his sword and put the point against the captive's chest lightly. "Repeat what you just told us."

Brom sat next to Zhuzak and listened as the terrified captive told the story again.

"We were supposed to ride to the capitals of Kalabria and its neighbors and kill the ruling families."

Zhuzak was about to say something, but Brom touched his arm, wanting the youth to continue, so Zhuzak turned to the captive.

"Tell him what is happening back at your main camp," he ordered.

"Mordin—he's the High Priest the prophet brought with him—has ordered the execution of the priest of Ost. He said the god is angry because the pilgrims had not found any glowing rocks and he says its the priest's doing."

Brom's eyes brightened. At least Mondlock was still alive.

"How many warriors remain in the camp?"

"There were more than five hundred when we left."

Brom turned to his men and shouted, "Who is ready to ride to save Mondlock and rid Kalabria of the vermin?"

A thundering cheer tore through the field as the warriors extinguished their fires, gathered up their belongings and started mounting their animals.

Zhuzak selected one of the men to ride back to Tella and lead the funeral preparers to the battlefield. Before the soldier could voice his protest, Zhuzak stopped him.

"That's an order. May another warrior do the same for you when you have fallen in battle."

The nervous captive looked up at Brom.

"What about me?"

"How fast can you run?"

"I don't know," the fearful youth mumbled. "Fast, I think."

"Then start running. If you are found in Kalabria after the next sun comes up, you will be stewed for our evening meal."

He watched the prisoner take off and run as if a demon were at his heels, then turned to Zhuzak.

"Let's ride."

Zhuzak paused. "Is Hogan coming?"

"He'll be here when the need comes," Brom said, "but in the meantime, we have to go on, so carry the flag before us."

23

Black Jack moved slowly. Ahead lay the ruins of the old monastery. Behind him, at the sagging wharf, a seaplane was waiting to take him back to the mainland.

In his hands Hogan gripped his favorite automatic rifle, the M-16A, loaded with Teflon-coated 5.56 mm rounds. Three full clips hung from his webbed belt, ready for grabbing. So did his 9 mm Beretta 91F and the Kalabrian long knife. A musette bag filled with extra clips for both weapons, grenades, plastic explosives and timers hung on his shoulder.

This was a sanctioned attack. From his hospital bed, Wilson had approved the action in the usual manner. If anything went wrong, the government would know nothing of Hogan's actions.

It seemed ironic to Hogan that in the last resort one man had to go up against those who endangered the whole world.

Most of the hirelings had been captured and the explosives they had planted had been deactivated, the hospitalized White House aide reported. All that remained was to capture the major actors in the plot.

As he approached the massive wooden doors, Hogan checked for signs of concealed gunmen. But the Aegean Sea washing against the wharf was the only sound reaching his straining ears.

It was too quiet. Where were the guards?

Steve had said he had flown ten middle-aged men here three days ago. Six of them had been escorted by armed muscle.

They had to still be here. There was no way off the small island except by plane or boat. And Steve would have known if a boat had come and taken them away.

The monastery itself was probably more than five hundred years old. Once it had been home for an order of Greek Orthodox monks. But no new monks joined to replace the ones who died, and for more than eighty years it remained empty. Then a year ago, a reclusive multimillionaire paid the church a huge sum to acquire the monastery and the island on which it stood.

That much Black Jack had gleaned from various sources. What no one could tell him was how the new owner had changed the interior.

A bad feeling closed in on Hogan as he gripped the huge metal handle on one of the doors. He had expected it to be locked, but it swing out effortlessly.

Something was definitely wrong. It had been too easy up until now.

He poked his automatic rifle inside, then jumped in and sideways, finding himself in a huge hallway. He swept his weapon in a quick arc, ready to fire at the enemy.

Dust was everywhere. Swirls of it spiraled in front of him as he moved into the building. He was tempted to sneeze but managed to contain himself.

Added to the musty smell, he detected another stench. The smell of the newly dead.

Hogan looked in both directions, then moved down the wide corridor in a crouch to a pair of wooden doors at the far end.

The silence was like cotton wool. Only the soft sounds of his feet moving carefully reached his ears. Holding his finger against the sensitive trigger, he kept turning from left to right to make sure no one emerged from a hidden door or corridor.

Then one of the doors at the end of the hall swung open. A man in monk's robes came into the corridor and nodded pleasantly.

"You are a difficult man to kill."

Hogan looked around quickly to make sure no hidden gun was preparing to change that statement.

"Your buddies have tried hard enough," Black Jack snapped.

"Unsuccessfully."

Hogan studied the man. His bright yellow hair spilled over the cowl of the hood on his robe. His eyes were like slanting almonds, intense and deep, giving his face a mysterious cast.

Hogan didn't really believe in sorcery. He had seen too many magicians and con men use sophisticated trickery to convince the gullible. But now he wasn't sure. The description of the so-called prophet from Kalabria fit the man who stood so calmly before him.

But how could he travel from this world to the other?

Then Hogan remembered that Brom and he managed to accomplish the same thing, though they didn't understand by what means.

Shrugging as he accepted the possibility that others besides the two of them possessed such an ability, Hogan said, "Your plan failed."

"Yes. The shortwave has been reporting that fact all day."

"The authorities know the men who were behind the plans," Black Jack added. "They want them."

The man tilted his head toward the open door.

"They're in there, along with the men who came to protect them."

Hogan wondered if he was being set up or if this was surrender. No previous encounter had gone this smoothly.

"You first," the American said, gesturing with his M-16A.

The man turned and walked into the room. Hogan followed and was stunned by what he saw.

The ten military leaders were at a rectangular conference table in the center of the room. The six bodyguards were sitting on chairs against a wall.

And all of them were dead.

They were sitting in their upholstered chairs, pads and pens on the table in front of each of them, staring sightlessly into space.

Containing his revulsion for the ten who had planned the mass destruction of millions of innocents, Hogan moved around the table, examining their bodies. There were no signs of wounds or pain.

He found Holaday's body at the head of the table. There was an expression of resignation on his face, as if the retired general knew what was in store for him and had accepted his fate.

For a moment Hogan understood how General Soong must have felt when he'd died before he could avenge his son's honor. Holaday was already dead so Black Jack couldn't make him pay for Charley Grisolm's death.

He studied the room for some clue to what had killed the men. There were no windows, just the pair of doors at each end. The fourteen-foot-high beamed ceiling was covered with undisturbed cobwebs.

There was no evidence that intruders had found a way to enter and kill the ten plotters and their guards.

There were carafes of water around the table, and half-filled glasses. On the floor next to their chairs, each of the guards had a similar glass of liquid.

"Hold it," Black Jack snapped as he moved to the table and picked up one of the glasses. He waved it under his nose. There was no odor.

Perhaps an odorless poison had been used. The American was aware that there were more exotic poisons and toxins available than he knew.

"What killed them?"

"Their failure," the man in the cleric's robes replied gently.

Hogan hated word games. "Tell what happened in plain English," he snapped.

"They failed. Therefore there was no longer a reason for them to live."

Hogan grew tense. Something was very weird about the conversation. "Who made that decision?"

"I did."

"How come you left yourself out of that decision?"

"It is not my destiny to die."

Hogan pointed his weapon at the man even as visions of the slain innocents at Harwood flashed into his head. "This says I can make it your destiny any time I want."

"Then shoot me."

"Come again?"

"I said shoot me."

Hogan wondered if he was facing a lunatic who thought he was impervious to bullets.

Suddenly the robed man walked to Hogan and shoved his finger inside the trigger guard. "Look well," he said. Leaning his body against the muzzle of the weapon, he forced Hogan's finger to push back on the trigger.

A loud burst of gunfire reverberated through the high-ceilinged room.

Hogan stepped back and stared at the other man. He was still standing there, apparently unscathed by the 5.56 mm round that tore through his midsection.

As the American kept on staring at him, the man turned and casually strolled to a door at the end of the room, opened it and went inside.

Hogan stood frozen in surprise for a moment, then decided he'd been exposed to some magician's trick and ran after him.

The large room was empty. A desk and leather chair against a wall and a massive time-stained mirror on the wall were the only furnishings.

Nothing else.

The yellow-haired man had vanished.

Hogan searched the room carefully for a hidden exit. But all the walls were solid stone, and the windows were too narrow to get through. The floors showed no sign of a trapdoor.

Hogan knew he was alone except for the dead men next door.

There was nothing he could do here. It was time to return to the living.

Hogan turned to leave, then glanced at the mirror. There was a reflection in it.

He moved closer. The faint outline of Brom looked out at him, but Hogan couldn't make out what was happening. The only thing he knew was that he was needed in Kalabria.

Gripping his M-16A tightly, he stepped forward, closing his eyes, and behind his eyelids he saw a play of light, then felt a sensation as though he were flying.

GRIPPING THE AK-47 he had brought back from Hogan's world, Brom stood alone on the crest of the hill and looked on at the vast encampment of pilgrims. Clusters of armed soldiers, no longer disguised by robes, wandered among them, prodding the exhausted men and women to their feet.

In long lines, they were being marched out of the camp and toward the desert that lay beyond their temporary home.

Bitter at the enslavement of innocents, Brom was tempted to charge right into the camp and slay the army of captors. Then he decided it would be wiser to put together a plan of action first.

He stared at the barren world of sand that stretched all the way to the distant mountains. The largest of the peaks was Mount Amatak where the gods dwelled.

Legend said their palace was inaccessible. Demons and fire-breathing dragons destroyed any who dared invade the area called the Forbidden Region.

Brom wondered what the enslaved men and women were supposed to find there. The only living things in that vast expanse were the poisonous Galiks and small rodents on whom they fed.

No plant life existed, not even the wild prickly weeds that could grow almost anywhere.

So intent was he in his survey that he hadn't noticed the archer who had climbed the hill behind him.

The bowman paused for a second, then slipped his weapon from his shoulder, and nocked a barb-tipped arrow in the gut bowstring. The bow formed a half-circle as he pulled the arrow back.

A loud explosion rang out and the archer fell forward, a stunned expression on his face. Where his back had been, there was now a gaping cavity from which blood spurted.

Brom whirled around at the sound and saw Hogan standing near the body. The American lowered his M-16A and strolled to the Kalabrian's side.

"Looks like I came just in time," he said as the two clasped forearms.

Brom studied the automatic rifle in the American's hands and the webbed belt cluttered with tools of destruction.

"You have come well prepared."

Black Jack glanced at the rifle the Kalabrian held. "Got any bullets left in that thing?"

"I am learning not to waste the death pellets needlessly," Brom replied with pride.

"Good." Hogan stared down at the encampment. "What's going on?"

"Slaves," Brom said with disgust, giving his red beard a fierce tug. "This so-called prophet has brought them to search for something out there." He pointed to the desert. "An insane adventure. There is nothing out there but death."

"What about Mondlock?"

Brom's face darkened. "He is being held prisoner in that camp." He showed Hogan a wooden scaffold erected by a group of men. "His execution is to take place this afternoon. He is to be crucified as a lesson to the others."

Hogan watched a tall dark figure in priest's robes come out of a tent and walk over to where the wooden platform was being constructed. He said something to one of the two guards who watched the workers.

"Who's that?"

"Mordin. A priest who takes pleasure in torturing women and infants. The man who calls himself a prophet has brought him to become the new High Priest of Ost."

"I wonder how the other priests of Ost will like that?"

"According to the soldier we questioned they are all dead. Mondlock is the last of the priests."

"What are we going to do? Stay up here and watch Mondlock be killed?"

"Not if I have any say in the matter," a new voice boomed.

Hogan and Brom turned. Zhuzak, the black-bearded commander of the Kalabrian troops grinned broadly as he wrapped his arms around Hogan.

"Good to see you again," Zhuzak beamed. "Lord Brom told me you would be here."

"Somebody has to help him rescue Mondlock and get rid of this prophet," Black Jack replied with a smile.

"I have torn powerful men to shreds with my bare hands for saying less than that," Zhuzak growled.

"As I remember, I won the last time."

"An error in judgment on my part. You were lucky."

"The error was made when you decided to wrestle with me," Hogan replied.

Quickly Brom stepped between the two. "Mondlock's execution draws nearer and you two stand here and bicker about a wrestling match," he said in reprimand.

Hogan and Zhuzak looked sheepish, then grinned at each other.

"We need a plan of action," the Kalabrian leader added. "There are at least five hundred of them and only a hundred of us."

Hogan turned his head and studied the camp below them.

"If you can get someone to cover me from the rear, I have an idea," he said.

"I will go with you," Brom announced.

Hogan opened his musette bag and took out a strange object. "My friend," he said to Zhuzak, "I'll tell you exactly how to use this wicked magic." Then he gave a quick rundown of his plan, and with Brom's approval, they were ready to penetrate the Forbidden Region.

24

Brom's troops were ready for a final battle with the prophet and his soliders, but the outcome hadn't been certain until Hogan had arrived. He had some surprises at hand, and with the brave Kalabrian warriors and the fierce Brom, he felt that they had a chance to win this battle.

The enemy was strong, fired by the hypnotic message of the prophet who had brought them, along with the innocent pilgrims, to the godforsaken region. The prophet was looking for the great god Ost, but the soldiers mainly wanted to be paid and stay in one piece. Still, they were in awe of the prophet and the awesome power he had displayed. Those who had dared to challenge his authority ended by killing themselves. There was no escaping the penetrating gaze, and everyone was resigned to the fight ahead. Or so some of the deserting soldiers from the enemy camp had said.

Before the day was over, a lot of blood would be shed, Hogan acknowledged to himself. In the early morning light, he could still see the twin moons in the sky. They were ready with their plan of attack against the invaders in the Forbidden Region.

Moving quickly between the tents, he worked his way to the roped area where the horses were kept. He glanced back. Brom, AK-47 in one hand and broadsword in the other, was right behind him.

Hogan paused and waited. After a few seconds he heard the explosion from the other side of the camp. Brom's man Zhuzak had followed his instructions regarding the explosives.

The guards turned at the loud thundering and started running. Black Jack pulled the pin, counted and pitched the oval metal at them as they came closer.

The grenade exploded, sounding like a hundred thunderstorms, and scattered its fragments of death. The horses neighed in terror at the violent noise, then charged at the ropes and tore past them.

In panic the animals broke into a gallop and rampaged through the camp in their desperation to escape.

From every corner of the camp, the soldiers ran to recapture their horses. Even the terrifying explosions didn't stop them.

A huge blond-bearded man grabbed the reins of his animal and tried to force it to stop. The frenzied creature reared up on his hind legs and flailed at the mercenary with its forelegs until the suddenly broken body released its hold on the leather straps.

Running through the swirl of frightened soldiers and their crazed mounts, a captain finally made his way to the prophet's tent. He was new to his position and uncertain about what he should do next.

"We're being attacked. The horses have escaped," he blurted out breathlessly.

The prophet was seated on a small stool. He appeared to be pale and exhausted.

In a corner of the tent, his bound captive, Mondlock the Knower, sat on the bare ground.

"Go and beat back the attackers. And recapture the horses," the prophet ordered impatiently as he raised a hand to his yellow hair. He held his head as though it pained him.

"Yes," the commander agreed. "That is what I should do."

He dashed out of the tent.

The prophet removed the gag that covered Mondlock's mouth. "The creatures of your world are less than intelligent," he said with resignation. "How you have managed to survive for so long is a mystery."

"The will of the gods," the wise man answered.

"There are no gods. There are only the living and the dead and nothing else."

"If you believe that, why do you keep the symbols of the priests of Ost? They are only harmless toys."

The prophet reached into the trunk and raised a handful of the medallions and studied them.

"Because they are so valuable to you. And they were to the other priests. Why?"

"It is a symbol of our faith in Ost."

"There is no Ost."

The sounds of gunfire from around the camp came closer, but the prophet did not flinch or blanch with fear.

"The Kalabrians don't have guns. Someone else is fighting with them. That creature called Hogan." He stared coldly at the wise man with eyes that looked older than time itself. "Who is this Hogan? How does he and your Lord Brom manage to survive?"

"It is written in the legends that two great warriors will come when the world is in need of them and save it from those who would destroy it."

"Fairy tales, old man."

"Hogan and Brom are not fairy tales."

"The real problem is," the prophet continued as though speaking to himself, "that I mainly have to act through others—usually inept. But these two have something more that I can't put my finger on. They are human, and yet . . ."

The robed man stopped and stared at his prisoner. "Tell me where the temple of Ost is, and I will leave this world to find its own future."

Mondlock didn't believe the words. But the thought flashed into his mind that he could delay some indescribable doom. "You hold the temple in your hand."

The yellow-haired man glanced at the medallion. "Do you take me for a fool?"

"Fools are those who don't see the obvious," Mondlock replied cryptically.

To the robed figure, only one thing was obvious. Time was running out. He had mere months left. But there were still thousands of worlds to explore for the desperately needed glowing rocks. He had to suspend his search on this and the other world. At least for now.

"I will take these medallions to remember you. And I will return," he promised, then turned and walked out of the tent.

OUTSIDE THE TENT, a huge battle raged. Kalabrian warriors and hired soldiers were in close-quarter combat. The swish of swords cleaving through air, the heavy thud of battle-axes were followed by the cries of the wounded.

As the press of straining bodies grew closer, short swords and knives came into play. Those who had lost their weapons used their bare hands.

Hogan saw a furious Kalabrian grab the head of a hired soldier and bite off his ear, then spit it out. Tearing the knife from the soldier's hand, the Kalabrian rammed it into his belly.

There was no organized campaign. Just brute force fighting brute force any way possible. The only thing that mattered was who lived.

Hogan and Brom had plunged into the midst of the battle. It was too close to use the M-16A, but Hogan's Beretta kept spitting death in every direction as he worked his way to the center of the camp. Their lives at stake, the enemy fought back desperately despite Black Jack's strange weapon and the awe it inspired in them.

Brom had dropped his fire-stick and slashed his way through the mass of bodies facing him with the sharp edge of his broadsword. Glancing to his left, he saw Hogan making his way in the melee. As the Kalabrian watched, a fallen soldier pulled himself to his feet and drew a curved dagger from his waistband. A mask of hate covered his face as he started to charge at Hogan's back.

There was no time for a warning. Brom drew his krall and threw it expertly. The honed tip tore into the left eye of the assassin and penetrated into his brain.

Hogan turned and saw the would-be killer fall.

"I still owe you one," he called out.

Then he saw the sun glint on the edge of a battle-ax in the hand of a figure creeping up on the red-bearded warrior. Without hesitation, Black Jack fired two rounds.

Hot lead ruptured the blood vessels in the neck of the ax-wielder, and the weapon flew from his hands.

It was Brom's turn to look back and see the body behind him. "Now we are even, Hogan," he shouted back, and forged ahead, his sword flashing in the light.

The dead and the wounded littered the ground amid crimson pools of blood. Slowly the sounds of battle started to recede.

Finally less than fifty of the hired soldiers were left. Looking around and seeing how small their numbers had become, they turned and ran from the camp before death could mow them down, too.

Zhuzak started to gather a group of warriors to pursue them, but a weary-looking Brom stopped him. "Let them run. They won't stop until they reach the Great Eastern Desert or die from trying. We've won the battle, and the warriors could use a rest."

Zhuzak nodded, then left to take account of dead Kalabrians.

Hogan walked slowly at the red-bearded warrior's side. He was covered with blood.

"I must wash this off myself," he said as he looked down at his body.

"First," Brom insisted, "both of us will present ourselves to the gods."

Black Jack was too tired to argue. "Where do we find them?"

Brom led him to the prophet's tent. "I am told this so-called prophet has stolen many of the statues of our gods. We should find some in here."

The two men entered the tent and right away saw Mondlock. After Brom untied him, he looked around.

"Where is the man who calls himself a prophet?"

"Gone. At least for now. He will soon discover that he has some of what he came to find," the Knower replied.

He fingered his neck where the missing medallion had hung.

Each of the heavy medallions contained a bit of the glowing rock from the sacred vessel in the temple of Ost. The thick metal kept their energy from escaping. The wise man was certain the prophet would learn their secrets.

As was sometimes the case, Mondlock's reply had confused Brom. But the wise man looked unharmed. "Is everything well with you, wise Knower?"

"I am weary but uninjured."

"Good. Then you can come back and save me from the hell of trying to rule," the Kalabrian leader said with relief. "Fighting is for men, but haggling over things is, well, for wise men."

He started to lead Mondlock from the tent, but Hogan stopped him. He looked decidedly unhappy.

"What about these gods you were going to present us to? You said I could wash after you did."

"Go and do as you please. You have already presented yourself before them," Mondlock said, then glanced at Brom. "Both of you have."

A faint shimmering appeared in the tent, and they stood silently for a minute.

"I guess I'll have to take that bath someplace else," Black Jack said. He winked at Brom. "Tell Astrah I'll be back."

"She will expect you soon," Brom replied. "So will I. My friend, it's you and I against whatever evil spirits fall upon our worlds. Hail, brave brother."

The Guardian Strikes

David North

A cloud of deadly gas is about to settle, and then a madman's dreams for a perfect society will be fulfilled. Behind it all is a sinister being searching for life-giving energy. He is the last of an ancient godlike race called the Guardians, and his survival hinges on the annihilation of the Earth's population.

Standing between him and survival are two men—the former CIA counterinsurgency specialist and the swordsman from the mists of time. Once again they join forces across time to defeat the savage being determined to destroy both their worlds.

Look for THE GUARDIAN STRIKES, Book 3 of the Gold Eagle miniseries TIME WARRIORS.

GOLD EAGLE

The Eagle now lands at different times at your retail outlet!

Be sure to look for your favorite action adventure from Gold Eagle on these dates each month.

Publication Month	In-Store Dates
September	August 21
October	September 25
November	October 23
December	November 20

We hope that this new schedule will be convenient for you.

Please note: There may be slight variations in on-sale dates in your area due to differences in shipping and handling.

GEDATES-1

**Raw determination in
a stillborn land...**

JAMES AXLER

DEATH LANDS®

Seedling

As Ryan Cawdor and his roaming band of survivors desperately seek to escape their nuclear hell, they emerge from a gateway into the ruins of Manhattan.

Under this urban wasteland lives the King of the Underground, presiding over his subterranean fortress filled with pre-nuke memorabilia. And here, in this once-great metropolis, lives Ryan Cawdor's son....

The children shall inherit the earth.
